I0757285

SANTE

DARK MAFIA BILLIONAIRE ROMANCE BOOK 2

L. K. RYAN

Copyright © 2021 by L.K. Ryan

All rights reserved.

No part of this book may be reproduced in any form or by any electronic or mechanical means, including information storage and retrieval systems, without written permission from the author, except for the use of brief quotations in a book review.

This is a work of fiction. Names, characters, places, and incidents are either the product of the author's imagination or are used fictitiously, and any resemblance to actual persons, living or dead, business establishments, events or locales is entirely coincidental.

For questions and comments about this book, please contact me at authorlkryan@gmail.com. Visit the official website at www.authorlkryan.com

Editor: Susan Soares

DISCLAIMER

Warning: There are a few scenes that may trigger. Be aware. Contains strong language and explicit sexual content and is only intended for mature readers. A dark mafia billionaire romance with an asshole alpha male, possessive, and aggressive. This story may contain unconventional situations, language, and sexual encounters that may offend some readers. This book is for mature readers (18+).

SYNOPSIS

In my capacity as underboss of the Calabresi Mafia, I was respected and held in the same high esteem as my brother Savio, the Don of the family. The decision he made caused a chain reaction, and I made the decision to clean it all up. Unfortunately, it came with six-inch heels, red lipstick, and a mouth that liked to push all my buttons.

A hate-to-love, enemies-to-lovers, arranged marriage, dark mafia romance, Book 2 in an interconnecting stand-alone series, and guaranteed to have an HEA.

INTRODUCTION

Are you signed up for my newsletter?

Join today and find out all the latest in new releases, contests, giveaways, sneak peeks and more.

CALABRESI FAMILY

Elio Calabresi-Father, Retired Don
Adelina Calabresi-Mother
Savio Calabresi- Boss
Sante Calabresi-UnderBoss
Renato Calabresi-Enforcer
EJ Calabresi-Consigliere
Vincenzo Calabresi: Calabresi Holdings Inc President

CHAPTER

ONE

SANTE

S avio sat with his back to us in the conference room of the Calabresi office, where he normally wouldn't have us discuss mafia business. After retaliation for Maurizio's murder on a few of our spots, we needed to discuss what the next move would be. To see my brother married and happy with a wife and baby in the near future was shocking for the entire family, but my mother hadn't stopped crying since the news was broken at a family dinner.

"How many warehouses did they hit?" He whipped around in his chair and looked my way.

As the underboss, it was my job to keep things running without causing him any distress, but lately, things had gotten out of control with Carmine now in position as the head boss for the Colombo Family.

"At least three."

"Three, Sante," he growled

"We need to strike back, or they'll think we're weak," Renato complained while he removed his gun from his holster.

"Put that gun away," I demanded.

"Nobody's in here."

"Renato, this is a palace of business." Savio pointed his finger to the table.

"I agree with Renato on this one," Elio J said.

"Usually, you're the one who wants less death," Savio replied.

"We can't be seen as weak. We already have Greco's team," EJ responded.

"You have to wait!" a loud voice called out.

The conference room door flew open, and Satan's spawn in six-inch heels narrowed her eyes on me. I didn't move; I only gave the same menacing look right back.

"You bastard!" Rena stalked around the table, and Renato blocked her pathway.

"Rena, this is a private meeting." Savio looked at her, then at me. All I could do was shrug. Her problems had nothing to do with me.

"No, let me go, Renato. Your brother is going to die today," Rena shouted and shoved Renato, but he wrapped his arm around her waist and held her back. I didn't like their closeness, so I motioned for him to let her go.

"Give me the room," I told them.

Everybody looked at me like I was crazy, and maybe I was, but she wasn't going to try to spin this around on me. Savio rose, and the rest followed. Renato whispered something in her ear, and she nodded, released his hold, and walked out.

"Speak."

"You got me fired."

"I didn't get you fired."

"Then tell me why I was told to clear out my desk."

Rena's bottom lip poked out, as she crossed her arms over her chest and glared at me.

"I had nothing to do with you getting fired. Excuse me, I have business to handle."

I walked around her, and she reached to grab my arm. My eyes scanned down at her grip.

"I know you got me fired."

"I don't have time to play childish games, little girl."

Suddenly, her bottom lip trembled, and tears gathered into her eyes. Savio and the rest of my brothers stared at each of us hard.

"We need to finish discussing business, Sante," Savio remarked, and I sat back down. They stepped in the conference room, and she paused, shook her head, and walked back out. I released a harsh breath and rubbed my temples to relax. I hated to get angry. Like Savio, I tried to suppress the beast inside me unless it was necessary.

"What was that about?"

"She thought I got her fired." I loosened my jacket.

"Did you?"

"Rena Clark is not important enough for me to get fired."

"But you tried to fight me when you thought she wanted to sleep with me," Renato recalled.

"That was different. I know your track record with women," I explained.

"You're just as bad, Sante," EJ blurted out.

"Fuck you, and let's get back to business."

"Do we know where Carmine's head is?" Savio probed.

"I think we need to keep an eye on him. Right now, they can't pinpoint that we made the hit, but we had the most beef with the Colombos." I leaned forward and explained.

"Keep me updated, but no more meetings here." Savio stood, shook hands with Renato, and hugged us both.

"Sante, hold up." The moment I arrived at the door, Savio called me by name.

"Yeah?"

"Is there anything going on with you and Rena?" Savio slid his hands in his pockets, standing tall.

"No."

"What happened when you had her held up in your apartment for those weeks?"

My teeth chattered as I recalled those first few weeks when he requested that I kidnap McKayla's best friend.

"Let's just say I'm looking into better security." I walked out of his office to catch up with Renato and EJ as they stepped on the elevator.

"What about the other thing?"

EJ pulled up his phone and passed it toward me. The door opened, and they followed me out the doors to our waiting car. I stared at the photos.

"Shit! We need to find another way." I grimaced, running a hand down my face.

Smack!

"Are you crazy!" I reached out to grab her, and EJ jumped in the middle of us, along with my bodyguard.

"You asshole! I'll get you for this," Rena shouted, pointing a finger in my face. People on the street watched us and pulled out their phones to record. I hated being the center of attention. She was embarrassing me and my family's name with her antics.

"Get this bitch out here before I do something she'll regret," I barked, shoving EJ away from me.

"Bitch! Ohhh, I regret the day I ever met you!" Rena screamed, reached for her heel, and tossed it at my head. I ducked before it hit me, and Renato laughed at us from the limo.

"Get—"

Pop! Pop! Rattata!!

Bullets sprayed the area from the windows of buildings, cars parked, and a few pedestrians.

"Rena!" I tried to grab her. EJ shoved me on the ground, and I failed to get over to her.

Pop! Pop!

The sounds stopped, and I jumped up and pulled my gun out, pointing toward the assailants driving off on a motorcycle. I was breathing hard, as the bike swerved around a corner before I could get a shot sent. It was hard to tell who thought it would be a good idea to come at us. We'd made moves to be untouchable.

"I have Vincenzo sending the video footage and the surrounding business to your phone," Renato exclaimed.

"Get off me!" Rena yelled, and I ran toward her and my bodyguard. He helped her stand up, and she brushed his hand away.

"Are you hurt?" I questioned, running a hand up and down her arms, and swerved her around.

"Don't touch me! This is all your fault, you bastard."

"Sante, we need to go," EJ told me, hopping in the limo.

"Make sure she gets home safe," I told the doorman of our building, and she glowered at me.

"I don't need anything from you."

"Rena, stop being a bitch and let the man help you."

She raised up her hand to hit me again, and I wrapped

a hand around her wrist to block her, pulling her into my chest.

"I don't give a damn if you're pissed. Get your ass in the car. I'd hate for McKayla to be upset and crying at your funeral because you've decided to ignore my help," I hissed, and the light in her eyes dropped in thought.

"Stay away from me," Rena spat, yanking her arm out of my grasp.

She limped over to the doorman, who escorted her to another awaiting car we had pulled up. Renato walked over to me with a harsh glare.

"What do you have?"

"Savio is making calls right now, but we think it's Carmine."

"You think, or it's for sure him."

The war I wanted to avoid was slowly seeping into our lives, and I didn't need Savio making any rash decisions. Now he was a married man with a baby on the way. I took more responsibility since McKayla needed him by her side.

Carmine was making himself known.

Renato slid a hand through his hair, and his eyes darkened with rage. I knew he hated being questioned, but as our enforcer, brother or not, his job was to see these things coming before they happened, so we could take precaution. I was grateful we acted in time and mostly everyone was safe, besides a few sore limbs. This was a big fuckup, and any other underboss would eliminate sloppiness from the team.

"I don't know for sure," he seethed, and we had a stare down.

"We don't have time for you two to go back and forth. Father wants us to report now," EJ demanded, and I broke our stare to get in the limo. Renato followed and closed the door. As the driver pulled off into traffic, I reached in my pocket for my cell phone to make a call.

"Where are you?" Savio questioned.

"With EJ and Renato, headed to see Pops."

"I'm here with Vincenzo. I called to check on McKayla. She's safe."

"Do you need us to swing by and pick up McKayla?" I ask.

Renato and EJ perked up when I mentioned McKayla.

"No, my men are already transporting her to the house. Make sure she doesn't worry," Savio explained.

"How long are you going to be at the office?"

"Shouldn't be too much longer. I'm waiting for all the footage to be downloaded."

"All right, keep me updated."

"Why do you sound off?"

Savio, as the big brother and boss, hated if things distracted us from our duties, and I knew if I lied, he'd be able to tell. I debated for a moment and figured to keep some details out of the equation.

"Rena was out there."

"What!" he shouted in my ear. I pulled the phone away.

"She's fine. Calm down, Savio."

"Where is she?"

"With our men, being escorted home."

"Do you know if McKayla finds out about this, it's going to stress her out," he barked.

That was all I'd been thinking about, not only our safety, but if something happened to McKayla and the baby, our parents would not only disown me, but Savio wouldn't care if I was his brother. Heads would roll, and

I'd be the first one on the chopping block to answer for the lack of protection.

"I'm handling it, Savio."

"Take the attitude out of your voice. Underboss or brother, my wife is number one priority, which means her best friend is to be safe at all times."

"I got it, *boss*," I answered and then heard the dial tone from him hanging up.

"Savio's pissed," EJ exclaimed, and I nodded, looked out the window as the limo arrived at our family home. This was our shelter when we were little boys, and now as men, we came to have not only a connection, but a discussion on what needed to be done in the best interest of the family.

I STARTED to slide the key in the door, and Cora suddenly pulled it open. She ran into my arms, and I knew she was scared and wanted to know what was happening. Growing up around us with her mom as our family cook, we all thought of her as a little sister.

She stood back and reached for Renato. She was the only woman, besides our mom and Cora's mom, who got any affection from Renato.

"I thought you three were dead." Cora wiped the tears stung her eyes.

EJ came in last. Cora gave him a hug, and he didn't reciprocate, which was strange. His eyes bounced from me to Cora as he reached an arm around her waist and rubbed her back.

"We're fine, Cora," EJ replied, releasing his grip. All three of us walked further into the house, and I stepped into the living room with my father talking on the phone.

"Where's Mom?" EJ questioned. Cora pointed to the kitchen. I walked further in the room to the fireplace, with the mantel covered in family photos of us as kids during the summer months in Italy.

"I need everything immediately covered by Tulio." Father ended the call, and a sigh escaped his lips as he pinched the bridge of his nose.

I placed the photo back down and faced him.

"Savio is getting the footage together," I said.

"You're the underboss. How did this happen, Sante?"

Father and I never had clashes the way he often did with Savio or Renato, but his questioning of my abilities would be the first time he'd see another side of me. I clenched my fists at my sides.

"We're looking into Papa."

His brows knitted together.

"Savio is handling the company, and his wife is pregnant. Did you forget!" he seethed, tossing his hands up and sitting on the couch. I marched over and took a seat next to him.

"My whole life has been in Savio's shadow, and I gladly do the job, but don't sit up here and make it seem like I've slacked in my duties, or did you forget Greco?"

"Sante."

I looked up at my mother. I approached and wrapped her in my arms, kissing her on the forehead.

"Madre."

She raised a hand to my cheek.

"Are you hurt?" She ran a hand down my chest, turning me around, and I chuckled.

"Mother, I'm fine."

She slapped me on the chest and wiggled her finger in my face.

"This is serious, Sante. Why am I getting calls on lockdown?" she fussed. My father reached a hand out toward her and pulled her down next to him.

Their love was the beacon of our family, like my grandparents before them. Even I knew that finding that bond would never happen for me. Savio joked often that I would be a recluse for the rest of my life because I lacked the emotional tools to connect with a woman outside of the bedroom. I explained my intentions head on, and they either wanted to do as I say or be replaced. At the age of thirty-four, I did everything that Savio did growing up, and he could now complain about my lack of relationships, but he was in my place once, until McKayla came around.

"We were leaving the office, but I have a feeling who's behind this."

"I cooked. Where's Savio?" she quipped.

"Still at the office, last time I talked to him." I glimpsed at my watch.

"What about McKayla?" Mother looked from me to my father.

"She's protected."

"I'll call." She jumped up, picked up the house phone, and dialed McKayla's number, heading out of the living room for privacy.

"Carmine is behind this," Father spoke slowly.

"I agree. After Maurizio's death, we knew he'd retaliate."

His cell vibrated along with mine.

Savio: *Here's the video*

"Turn on the news," I heard my father say. I reached

for the remote from the table and clinked to the local news station. A breaking news story broadcasted with a clip of me, Renato, EJ, and a bodyguard dropping down to the ground as stray bullets rained down on us. I gritted my teeth.

"Motherfucker!" I threw the remote across the room.

"Sante." Father glared at me.

"*We have breaking news with a local shooting at Calabresi Inc,*" explained by the reporter.

"This is not good."

All our hard work was based on being seen as a respectable family in the media. Our hands in legitimate business and gun smuggling would be compromised by this today. That was exactly what Carmine wanted.

"He planned for them to look at us as monsters."

"Tulio said to lay low. He's checking on statements from some of the people who were wounded." Father stood and shook his head. We'd come back from the book scandal, and now our names were being pulled into more issues.

"I say we kill him now." Renato leaned against the entrance of the door.

"I need to find out what he wants."

"Then what?"

"We bury him next to his boss."

Renato peeked behind him, then came closer to where I stood.

"Is Elio weird right now to you?"

"No, why?" I didn't want to say how I thought it was weird about his lack of comfort toward Cora.

"Nothing, maybe he's shook up."

"Listen, call a meeting with Carmine, the faster the better."

"If he declines?"

"Mandatory. If he doesn't show, that means he's showing how guilty he is, and I don't take betrayal easily."

"That's the Sante I remember." Renato grinned. I flipped him off, and we hugged each other.

"I want our men surrounding the building, even across the street with snipers."

"Have you talked to Savio about your idea?"

"I will."

"If he finds out later, you know he'll hate to be left out of the loop."

We started toward the kitchen together.

"Once things clear up, and I get some sleep, I'll have a meeting with just the four of us."

"Father knows about your proposal?"

"No one except you, and I'm trusting you to support the deal."

He raised his hands.

"Anything that brings me more money and guns, I'm all for the setup."

I wrapped my arms around his shoulder and came into the kitchen with my mother laughing with Cora and Father.

"Where's EJ?" I probed.

"Somewhere around here, pouting," Mother declared. I stared at Cora for a brief second and saw she ignored the question and packed up her bags.

"Hey, where are you going?" I asked.

"Home, you guys are safe now."

"No one leaves Cora."

"Sante," Cora whined, throwing her hands on her hip.

"He's right, Cora. What if they're still watching?" Mother dropped the knife on the counter.

Cora sighed, rolling her eyes at me, removed her bag, and went to sit at the island.

"Besides kids, you have people at the office to handle things. If something happens to you, your mother would kill me." I patted her on the head, and she pushed me away.

"Sante, that's not the point I'm in charge of," Cora grumbled, picked up the tomato, and helped my mother to prepare the salad.

"What did McKayla say?" I snatched a piece of the tomato from the pile and tossed it in my mouth.

"She's with Rena, and they're okay. Savio arrived home, while Vincenzo wanted to get things fixed at the office."

"I'm going to head out and make some calls."

"Me too." Renato kissed our mother and Cora on the cheek and followed me out of the kitchen.

"Keep me updated, boys!" Father called to our backs.

I gave a thumbs up and continued out of the house and hopped in my car that I kept at my parents' house.

"Am I dropping you off?" I asked Renato.

"No, my men are coming, and we're going out to check on some things."

I slammed my door, started the car as the gate doors opened, and Renato's crew pulled up.

"Call if anything happens."

"You just remember to call a meeting." He walked backwards to the car and jumped in the passenger side.

"Try not to end up in jail!" I shouted.

"Jail can't handle me!" He laughed, as they turned on the roundabout and turned left.

CHAPTER
TWO

RENA

Tossing the towel on the bed, I strolled out of the bathroom with my lotion in hand. Today had been a day I didn't expect. When I confronted Sante about getting me fired, he wanted to play it off, but I knew he was a sneaky bastard when I saw one. Samira told me that I was let go because I showed up late too many times and received complaints. *Who does something so childish and gets a person fired?* McKayla thought I was crazy for going up there and confronting him, but I didn't give a damn what he thought or how I looked in front of his brothers or staff. This job was all I knew and what I loved to do. Growing up, I wanted to be a designer and make all my clothes. My brother and I grew up without our father, and the pressure put on my mom to get us through school was hard on her. I liked to take in those times and be grateful because they made me a stronger person who didn't take shit from anyone. I dropped the robe and scanned my body again. Even though no bullets hit me, I still dropped to the ground fast and scarred my leg.

"Here you go. Rena, please put some clothes on." McKayla shook her head and passed the tray of soup and a bottle of water to me. I called her on my way home and checked if she could sit with me. At first, Savio was against her leaving the house, but McKayla told him she'd sneak out if he didn't agree, but he did force her to drive over with the entire military force.

"Why? This is my house and bedroom." I planted my hands on my hips, tilting my head to the right.

"I'm a guest, and we have bodyguards in the living room."

"Who cares? They'll welcome a little T&A for a change compared to today's events."

She waved me off and sat on the bed, rubbing her stomach.

"Tell me again what happened."

I groaned and stomped over to the closet to pick out a short shirt set to change into.

"I confronted Sante in the office about getting me fired, then left."

"Are you positive he was the one who got you fired?"

"Who else would have done it, McKayla?"

"Be honest with yourself. You really didn't like the job."

"Honestly, as my best friend, you should be on my side." I grabbed my brush and combed my hair into a ponytail away.

"Where are you going?"

"To my mom's."

"How is she doing?" McKayla reached her hand out for help to stand. I ran a hand across her pregnant belly.

"How far along are you now?"

"Eight months." McKayla blew out a breath.

"Is Savio ready for fatherhood?"

"He has no choice. All this is his fault," she joked. I grabbed my purse and sauntered out of my room.

"Surprised he let you out of the house."

"I threatened to sneak out."

I grasped the knob, and a guard jumped up and blocked me.

"Miss Clark, we have instructions to keep you inside."

"On whose orders?"

"Mr. Sante."

I cocked my head at McKayla.

"How am I being forced to stay in my apartment when I've done nothing wrong and have no relationship to this family?"

"Rena maybe call her."

I stomped my foot.

"No! You might let them run your life, but I don't, McKayla. This is ridiculous. Move out of my way." I tried to push him aside, but he didn't budge.

"We can't let you do that," he replied, cuffing his hands.

I reached in my purse and pulled out my gun and pointed at him, McKayla gasped.

"Rena!"

"Either you move on your own, or I move you myself."

He held up his hands in surrender, and I smirked.

"Thank you." I opened the door and walked out.

"Rena, hold up!" McKayla shouted. I poked my head back in the apartment.

"Ma'am, we can't let you go. She's not Savio's wife, so we can't force her," he declared, blocking her from leaving.

"Don't worry, I'll call you later." I blew her a kiss and headed to the awaiting car service I had ordered earlier.

"Where to, ma'am?"

"Home to Naperville."

Ring!

Sante: You pulled a gun on my men?

I chuckled and replied.

Rena: Yep.

Sante: Are you fucking crazy?

Rena: Yes and I told you that the first time you kidnapped me.

∽

"WHAT, SANTE?" *Savio groaned.*

"I'll take her friend to my place."

"What?" Rena and I said at the same time.

"Are you kidnapping now?"

He motioned his hands out.

"It hasn't worked out for you so far."

"Whatever, Sante. Take her and keep her out of the public eye until I can decide what to do with her."

The guy Sante went to grab Rena, but she pushed him away and stood.

"Listen Rena, just do what they say, and I'll call you," McKayla spoke, under a shaky breath.

"We can call the police, McKayla."

An hour later, I was pushed into his apartment, with a gun to my back, as he talked to his men and brought my things.

"You'll be here for a few days until we close the deal."

"You can't keep me locked like I'm in prison, Sante."

He glowered at me. I charged toward him and lifted my hand to punch him in the face, but he gripped my arm, blocking me.

"Stop fighting me!" he yelled, pulling me back to his chest. Our chests rose and fell, our breaths hitched. I pulled his hand to my mouth and gripped down tight.

"Bitch!"

He pushed me off him, but I kicked him in the balls. Watching him drop to the floor, I started to climb over him to get the door opened, but he grasped my leg and reached to grip my hair.

"Argh!"

"Boss!" His men came from outside and pulled us apart as he seethed with rage.

"Take her to the guest room and lock her up," he demanded.

"Let me go!"

"Take her phone and clothes, and no food."

My eyes widened in shock.

"You can't do that." My stomach dropped at his statements.

He cocked his head to the side.

"Have to make sure your prison stay is an authentic, Miss Clark."

I kicked my leg out again to hit him, but the guards dragged me to the bedroom. Once locked inside, I banged on the door.

"I'll call the police! Let me out of here now."

I slammed my hand on the door and crawled down to the floor with tears stinging my eyes. The guest room was large with a queen-size bed, TV, and bathroom. I should be happy he didn't hurt me too badly, but it was only a matter of time before one of us killed each other.

As THE CAR pulled up to my mother's home, I closed out my messages and blocked Sante to avoid another situation of back and forth arguing.

"Thanks for the ride." I gave him forty dollars and closed the door behind me.

My mother had only been in this house for the past ten years after my brother got elected and made it as a congressman. When he told us what he wanted to do, I thought he was crazy and lost his mind, being in the public eye like that, but he wanted to give my mother a better life. I put my key in the door, it chimed, and I heard laughing that made me feel like I made the right decision to stay here and recuperate away from everything.

"Rena! Honey, why didn't you call?" Mom placed her glass of wine down and pulled me into her arms.

Darla Clark was the rock of our family and the only person I trusted besides McKayla with my life. She'd been my confidant, teacher, and friend in my corner, who got me and my brother through the rough times once our dad walked out on us.

"It was a last-minute thing. Did you cook?"

"I would have fixed up your room if I knew."

I dipped a wooden spoon in the sauce and tasted the spicy flavors on my tongue.

"What are you cooking?" I avoided answering her question.

She tapped my hand to drop the spoon, picked up the plate, and poured sauce and noodles on a plate with a fork.

"Last time I talked to you, McKayla was getting married and pregnant."

"She's eight months old now."

"Wow, that's great. Send her my love."

"I will." I removed my purse and put it on the counter.

"So."

"What?"

"Why are you here?"

I dropped my fork.

"Why can't I just come to see my mother?"

"You can always come home, but I know my child and you've never just dropped over without notice."

She sat next to me on the island, as I looked around the kitchen and saw the updated renovations she'd made on the kitchen.

"I lost my job."

"How? You loved that job."

"Someone got me fired."

"What! Who?"

"It's not important."

"Anything that happens to you is important. Do I need to call you brother?"

My brother thought of me as the screwup, even if he didn't show it in front of my mom. He was the oldest at thirty-six. I, however, being thirty with a desk job that, according to him, wasted tax payers dollars with lies.

"No, leave it alone."

Her brow hiked in suspension.

"Rena, tell me what's going on."

"Nothing is going on. I need to get some sleep and look for a job tomorrow."

"How long are you staying here?'

I took the last bite of spaghetti and picked up her bottle of wine to pour myself a glass, gulping it down.

"I have enough savings to cover my apartment for six months, so I might as well cut the lease now and move back here."

"Okay, get some rest for the night, and we'll pick this up tomorrow."

"You've always made the best spaghetti."

"Glad I could feed you. Now finish up, then get some rest." She hugged me again, and we chatted over her friends' problems with their kids.

"I remember when you used to dye your hair, and it would be all over the counter and your clothes," she reminisced, and I laughed.

"I found my color red and haven't changed it since."

"No men in your life?"

"Nope."

Knock! Knock!

"Who that be? Are you expecting anyone?" She wiped both sides of her mouth and headed to the front door.

"McKayla is the only one who knows where I am."

"Maybe that's her!" she called out, opening the door.

"Hello, is Rena is here."

I choked on my wine at the sound of his silky-smooth voice. *How did he know I would come here?* I jumped out of my seat, slid to the side of the wall, and peeked down the hall to see if it was him and pulled back.

"Shit!" I went to the back door with my purse and opened it slightly to make it seem like I left. The house was two stories with a basement, so I slipped in the side door and locked it behind me.

"She is. Can I ask who you are?"

"Sante Calabresi."

"Oh, are you Savio's brother?"

"Yes, ma'am."

I heard the voices getting louder.

"She's right here... Rena!"

"Did she drive here?" Sante asked. I heard a chill in his voice.

"No, a car service. Has something happened?"

"I'm sorry to say, but Rena's stolen money from my family," he lied. My blood was boiling, and I was ready to give him a reason to get shot since they missed earlier.

"Rena would never steal from anyone," Mom told. I felt a nervous tightening in my throat.

"That's what I thought, but some information was found that points to her."

"Is this why she was fired?"

I opened the door. "No!" I shouted, marching in the kitchen. My mother didn't see the smirk on his face, and I wanted to completely wipe it off with my gun.

"Rena, what's going on?" Mom asked.

"Nothing, he's leaving."

"Actually, I came to take you with me." His eyes were fixed upon me.

"I'm not going anywhere with you."

"The police were called, Rena. I'd hate to press charges."

"Wait, maybe we can pay it back. How much was it?" Mom went to grab her checkbook.

"He's lying, Mom."

"Ten million dollars isn't something I would lie about, *cara.*"

He'd used Italian when I lived with him for those few weeks, and he had taught me some words, and cara meant *dear.* That was his favorite to use on me when I pissed him off or made him laugh. Right now, nothing was funny. The measures he was taking to get me out here only meant he would kill me to cover up the shooting today. My only concern was my mother and how she would be treated once they got rid of me.

CHAPTER

THREE

SANTE

One hour earlier

She hadn't returned my text after my men informed me she drew a gun on them at her apartment. I'd gotten the call from Renato to meet up so after I went home showered and changed, I came straight to our warehouse that we deliver. Her grit and fire were something to be admired, but she was picking a fight with a lion that got its prey once it sensed fear, and Rena feared me, which she faked by being the first to manipulate the situation in her favor. After our first, I was in my condo, and she bit me and kicked me in the balls. I told Savio I wanted to kill her, that he'd better take her before one of us didn't leave alive.

"Sante, what do you think?" EJ questioned

"Sante!" Renato shouted.

"Yeah." I rubbed my chin and sat up in my seat.

"You have the floor," Alvize announced.

The top heads of each family sat together to hear the details of the shooting today. Carmine sat nonchalantly,

24

and I was ready to kill him, but we'd had enough heat on us since Nevo and Maurizio's killing.

"Carmine, I called you here to get clarification on today."

"What sort of clarification do you need?"

As I rubbed my tongue over my top teeth, I tried to control my breathing.

"Someone shot at Calabresi Inc offices. You wouldn't happen to know about that, would you?"

"We're still rebuilding after Maurizio's death." His nose flared.

"Sante, as you know, things have shifted, and you've taken on more responsibility from Savio. Are you sure or do you have proof it was Carmine seeking refuge for Colombo Family?"

"I don't need proof, Alvize. Carmine and I have had a past. Now that his boss is gone, he's trying to step up and play with the big boys."

He stared at me, and I shifted my gaze to EJ. He pressed the projector, and photos came up of the men from today's shooting.

"Gentlemen, as you can see, we've enlarged the photos."

"What is this?"

Ring!

I peeked at my phone.

"I have to take this." I got out of my seat to answer the phone.

"Boss, she's gone."

"Who?"

"Miss Clark."

I shifted my weight and looked behind me at everyone waiting for me to end the conversation.

"Where's McKayla?"

Savio informed me that McKayla was hanging with Rena once she got home to make sure she was okay. To hear that Rena's skipped out and if something happens to McKayla for tagging along I'd end up in a war with my brother.

"Have you talked to Savio?"

"He's already picked up McKayla." I closed my eyes, thankful she didn't follow Rena's stupidity. Sometimes it made me wonder how those two became friends. McKayla was sweet, funny, and sensible. Rena, on the other hand, drove me up a wall of madness.

"Sante!" EJ called my name, I covered the phone and turned to him.

"We need to reschedule."

"Where are you going?" Renato asked, as I walked out of the warehouse and jumped in my car.

"Get her phone location and send it to me." I ended the call and tossed the phone in the holder.

"Where the fuck are you running off to?" He held my door open.

I glanced at the men as the guards led them out.

"Keep an eye on Carmine. I have to take care of something."

"Is it family?"

"Rena."

"You need me to come with you?"

"No, just follow Carmine and keep me posted." Renato closed the door and walked off.

"Renato!" I yelled through the window.

His eyes were fixed on me.

"Don't tell Savio."

In response, his brows dipped low.

"Why?"

"I don't have time to explain."

"Savio's the boss."

"And I'm the underboss, so don't question me!" I hissed, put the car in drive, and pulled off down the road.

PRESENT TIME

I got her location texted to me from my team. To find out she was at a house I didn't know about pissed me off. I didn't know her information when we originally kidnapped her, so I made it my business to get everything about Rena Clark and her family.

"Get in the car," I shot back, my eyes glittering with anger.

Rena stood at the passenger door, and I blocked her from leaving. I had cars of men behind and in front, keeping their eyes around the area. I told Renato to put some people in her house going forward. Her slim, dainty nose scrunched up with her cool, olive skin tone, fiery red hair, and hazel eyes, daring me to challenge her.

"Did I not make myself clear earlier? Stay away from me." A flush stole into her cheeks.

As I bit into my teeth, I tried to tame my anger.

"We might have gotten off on the wrong foot. I'm not Savio. Get in the fucking car."

I moved in close, as she dropped her arms down to her side. Blinking, I looked down at her balled fists.

"If anything happens to my mother..."

Her words sank in, then she turned and got in the car.

The car was completely silent as I headed in and out

of traffic. I glanced in her direction, and she was texting on her phone.

"Why did you pull a gun on my men?"

She ignored my question.

"Are you listening to me?"

Another silent moment. I reached over the seat, snatched her phone, and rolled down my window to toss it in the street.

She gasped in shock.

"What is your problem!"

"You!" I shouted, swerving at the light, and pushed the gas faster.

"Take me home." Her mouth was tightly pursed.

"You are to stay put until I tell you to leave."

"Unlike you, I have to look for a job."

"Then take up a hobby, but you're not leaving."

I pulled up to her apartment.

"I was planning to stay at my mother's house."

"Why?"

"Because I... Never mind." She unlocked the door, slammed it shut, and stomped off to her apartment. I ran a hand down my face and gripped the steering wheel as she disappeared in the building. My head security guard stepped to my car.

"I shifted some people so I'll keep an eye on her."

"Good. Soon as we figure out if Carmine is behind this, we can leave her alone."

"Are you heading home?" he questioned.

"Yeah. I need to get things under control with the Colombo Family."

"I'll be there to drive you in the morning."

"Keep an eye on her."

He backed away from my car and headed to her building, and I turned into traffic, trailed by associates following me home. Thirty minutes later, I parked and walked to the penthouse in my secured building. After opening my door and removing my tie, I dropped my keys on the kitchen counter and opened the fridge but didn't see anything I wanted. I took off my jacket, unbuckled my cufflinks, and pushed the door open to my sanctuary. My master bedroom was decorated in white and blue, with a king-size bed and a balcony. The bathroom was as big as the living room with his and her sinks, a shower and a tub, separated by a wall. I dropped my pants in the hamper of dirty clothes and turned the water on to the highest temperature. Letting the water run down my face and over my head, I thought about the next moves we'd need to make. Ten minutes later, I walked out of the bathroom wrapped in a towel around my waist, stepped in my room, and slid under the covers, zoning out from an exhausting day.

Buzz!

I picked up my phone from the nightstand and saw a photo of Carmine with some guys on a corner. I placed it back on the charger and fell into a deep sleep as I figured how Carmine would come at us next.

FOUR

SANTE

Two days later

I slammed the documents down on the table and paced back and forth in front of my desk at Calabresi Inc. Not only was the news creating a massive narrative with this shooting in front of the building, Elio brought over the proof that Carmine was moving in on us. When the decision was made to get rid of Greco, then Maurizio, it was a risk. Somehow, they'd been able to convince a few people in high places that things were getting out of control.

"Did you tell Savio?" I probed, staring out of the window and sipping my coffee.

"Not yet; there's more."

I swiftly turned toward him.

"What else?"

"Did you read Rena's background?"

"No. It's in my safe at home."

EJ looked uncomfortable with what to share.

"Carmine knows about Rena."

"What do you mean he knows?"

Elio rested his hands on the arms of the chairs, leaning forward.

"Look, Sante, if you do this deal, we need to make sure you'll be protected."

"I agree."

"I think we need to talk to Papa about this to confirm we can pull this off."

I shook my head, placing my cup down as I sat on the edge of my desk.

"If I pull this off, I will be on another level and bring in even more money."

"Tell Savio and if he approves, then you have my vote."

"What about Rena's background?"

"Her brother is a senator."

"Why am I just hearing this now?" I jumped up and walked around my desk to pick up my cell and send a text to my security team.

"We were too focused on Carmine."

"Fuck!" I slammed my fist on the desk.

Ring!

I picked up the phone, and he didn't wait for me to speak.

"Come to my office," Savio demanded, and my eyes bounced from the phone to Elio.

"I'll be there in a second."

"Savio," EJ said, standing.

When the call ended, I looked down at my desk, rage brewing in my stomach. Carmine would pay for fucking with my family.

"He wants to meet in his office."

"McKayla had a doctor's appointment yesterday," EJ informed me, and I closed my computer down, scooped up my phone, and left my office to head toward Savio's office.

"Don't force my hand," Savio scolded, slamming the phone down.

EJ and I stared at each other, then him.

He pointed at the chairs in front of his desk.

"Sit and tell me why I'm having to clean up your mess, Sante."

I released a sigh of frustration at being called out in front of my little brother. Savio knew the bullshit I put up with him growing up in his shadow and the stupid decisions he made.

"I underestimated Savio."

"What did you find out about Elio?"

"I was filling Sante in on the fact that Carmine is behind the shooting in retaliation for Greco and Maruizio."

"What else?" Savio leaned back in his chair and watched me.

"Sante set up the plans for the gun export."

"A gun import and export deal that I didn't know about," Savio expressed.

"Since when do I need to run everything by you?"

"The fact you have to say that tells me your head is getting as big as underboss."

I waved him off.

"You've finally cut down on your conquests with women getting more focused on business and you do something like this."

"How was McKayla's appointment?"

A foolish distraction, but a glimmer of a smile crept up at the corner of my lip.

"She's good, and the baby's healthy."

"Did you figure out a name yet?"

"No, we have a few names written down, but we can't decide."

"You'll come up with something that represents our heritage."

"Your questions don't stop me from wanting an answer, Sante."

"The deal I'm trying to get pushed through is having the senator agree to vote on a bill that will allow our business to be tied in with trucking."

"Tell me more."

"What does America love more than money?"

"Power," Elio replied and nodded.

"If we get the vote, the transportation bill will include funding for a host of companies that deal in trucking across the East Coast."

"Which would make our gun business viable and more powerful."

"Where all the families will need to come to us because they will control the import and export."

"Who is the holding senator?"

Elio cut his eyes at me.

"Ted Clark."

"Who's Ted Clark?"

"Rena Clark's brother."

Savio sat up in his chair, cocking his head to the right.

"You've made contact with him?"

"Not yet."

"We've only gotten backgrounds on all the senators so far," EJ explained. By this time, I'd made up a reason to get him on board and kill Carmine at the same time.

"Does she know that we know?"

"I doubt it."

"McKayla can't know about this."

"Are you approving the deal? It could mean over ten million dollars."

"Keep my wife out of whatever you're planning."

"I have a plan to get him to vote."

"What's the plan?"

"Carmine knows we've been snooping around to gain more control, after Maurizio's death."

"He figured out we made the call," Savio answered, and I nodded.

"The shooting was a warning. If we keep pushing the vote, he's going to come for us."

"So, it's about money more than revenge," Savio quipped.

"That's what Elio suspects." I pointed at EJ.

"How will you get Ted onboard?" Savio questioned.

"Kill him or Rena," I announced.

The heads of both Savio and EJ shot around me.

I BLEW out the smoke from the cigar as I sat in the VIP section of the nightclub with dancers moving in front of me. Savio thought I was insane for even thinking of a plan like killing Rena. He'd become attached and thought of her as a sister. We ended up fighting, and I came here to unwind and have a drink. Renato followed me after EJ called him once they broke us apart. All he was worried about was McKayla, which I understood, but she didn't need to know everything.

"Sante, can I go home with you tonight?" Gaileia stood in front me only wearing a thin strappy, gold dress, with her breasts spilling out. I'd hooked up with her before, but she grew attached too fast, and I cut her off.

"Not tonight, Gaileia."

"Why? I know the deal. I won't tell." She bent down and whispered in my ear. I ran my finger across her full breasts, up to her chin.

"Go pick up another drink, Gaileia. I need to talk to my brother." Renato grabbed the bottle of tequila and placed it back in the bucket of ice. I glared at him, lifting the cigar to my lips.

"We're fighting each other now?"

"He overreacted." I pushed the cigar out in the ashtray and lit another one.

The base of the music engulfed the room, and I watched another dancer on a pole kick her legs up and bounce on the pole. It was more of gentlemen's club rather than a nightclub, where women could get naked from the top up. I invested in the club as a silent partner but didn't come here that often. Besides Calabresi Inc, I made money from investments in businesses I could see potential growth. Rena said that the comment about the loss of her job wasn't completely a lie. I didn't get her fired. I ordered Elio to make the call. I chuckled at the thought of her face when she marched in the conference room.

"That's why you have a black eye forming," he quipped, and I flipped him off.

"You think we can flip Ted."

"He has no choice."

"The deal with the Serbians would triple if we can pull this off."

Rena was working on a story at her newspaper that involved political corruption from outside forces. It was just a matter of time before she put the dots together, and now hearing about her brother Ted being a senator brought more challenges to this vote.

"McKayla called our mom and told her about the fight," he summarized, and my eyes bucked in surprise.

"Savio must have explained his busted lip."

"You have Elio going crazy, almost having a heart attack." Renato chuckled.

I shrugged my shoulders, grabbed the tequila again, and poured a shot.

"Have a drink with me."

"Nope. I'm here to take you home."

"Not ready."

"Doesn't matter, we're still dealing with Carmine's men."

"Carmine isn't stupid."

"Did we not just deal with a shootout two days ago?"

"It was a warning. Carmine will be dealt with soon."

He snatched the bottle and glass out of my hand.

"Let's go," Renato demanded, and my eyes dipped low.

"I'm the big brother."

"Then act like the brother that I grew up admiring and wanting to be like."

I stumbled as I stood.

"Fuck you."

"Save that for Rena." My shoulders stiffened when I heard those words of Rena having sex. It was stupid because we hated each other. I despised everything about her, but hearing her name come out of his mouth pissed me off.

"I can get home myself."

"Do you want me to close this place permanently?"

Renato pushed his coat to the side and showed his gun. I grabbed the bottle out of his hand, took another shot, and left the VIP section, tapping my guards to let them know I was ready to leave. I took my keys out of my pocket, pushed the door of the club open, and hit the unlock button on my key fob.

Bomb!

The force of the explosion pushed me across the parking lot a few feet, and I landed on my back. Hearing voices around me, I felt soreness from the impact, and a bad headache was brewing. Fire blazed in front of us as people came out of the club, talking on the phone and taking pictures.

"Sante!" Renato ran toward me yelling my name.

As I slid up on the side of the wall, he lifted me around his shoulder to help me stand.

"Are you hurt?"

"No, just sore."

The sirens from the fire trucks as they approached, blocking of the street and bringing out water hoses. Renato walked me to his car and opened the door.

"Hold on. I will get you to our doctor."

I grimaced, holding my chest as I slid in slowly with blood dripping down my nose. Renato ran to the driver's door.

"Follow us to his place!" Renato called out as he drove through the back alley and down the street to avoid the police. My eyes were getting low, and I felt like I needed to sleep.

"Hang on, Sante." Renato tapped me on the cheek, and I nodded.

"Shit! My ribs hurt." I tried to sit up.

"Don't move. I'm going to kill his ass." Renato slapped the steering wheel.

"Carmine is more dangerous than Greco and Maruizio combined."

"He's bold to do this stunt."

Fifteen minutes later, we arrived at my condo, and Renato parked in front and jumped out to have the valet to move it for them. I slowly stepped out as our doctor approached me, helping to get on the elevator and up to my penthouse.

"What happened?" Doctor Ira helped me to lie down, checking my temperature and heart rate.

"Explosion."

"Anyone else hurt?"

"I don't know," I muttered.

"You don't seem to have any major injuries."

"I'll be fine. Just give me something for my head." I went to sit against the headboard, and Ira nudged me back down.

"I want you to be monitored for the next day or two," Ira requested, took the bottle of water out of Renato's hand, and placed the aspirin in my hand.

"Too much going on to be on bedrest."

"It's for your own good, Sante."

I swallowed the pills and relaxed as he patched up my ribs.

"Doc, is he going to be good?" Renato questioned.

He stood and placed his gear in his bag. As the family doctor, he'd been around since I was a child.

"He'll be fine. Remind him to take it easy." Doctor Ira pointed at me and left the bottle of pills on the side table.

"Renato, make sure the doctor is compensated. I'm

going to sleep." I went to turn on my side but froze from the pain.

"Call me tomorrow," Renato said.

"Keep this to yourself," I mumbled, dosing off to sleep as the door closed.

CHAPTER

FIVE

RENA

A week later

The last time I spoke to my mom, she wanted to come over to my place to check up on me, but I avoided an answer. Things were difficult enough with me not working. Right now, I needed to figure out my next steps and keep my distance from the entire Calabresi Family if I wanted some type of normalcy. McKayla called a few times over the past few days. We talked briefly, and she told me that they'd decided on a baby's name. Even Savio's mom called to check up and apologize for Sante's behavior.

Knock! Knock!

I jumped up off the couch and looked out the peephole before I opened the door. A wide smile covered my face.

"Nikki! When did you get to town?" I hugged her tight, then pulled back to see her holding shopping bags in her hand.

"Can I come in?"

"Yes, of course, please." I stepped aside to allow her

entry. I noticed guards still standing in place. As I kicked the door closed, I watched her place them on the table near my work. I went to the kitchen for a bottle of wine.

"I have wine if you're thirsty."

Nikki was one of my best friends growing up, and she lived in New York for work as a fashion assistant at a high-end boutique that catered to celebrities.

"Pass me the whole bottle," she joked, pulling out a long beautiful black leather dress.

I poured half a glass of wine for us both.

"What are you doing in town?"

"You."

I pointed at myself and sat on the edge of the couch.

"How did I inform you to come back?"

"I heard about you not working at the paper anymore."

There was no luck in hiding my jobless situation, and I didn't like sympathy from friends or a handout.

"How did you hear?"

"I called the paper looking for you."

"I bet she couldn't wait to throw me out," I chortled, drank the rest of the wine, and poured more in the glass.

"It doesn't matter, but I think we need to go celebrate."

"Celebrate..." In confusion, I raised my eyebrows.

"What you need is a day of pampering and a night of flirting."

"What is that like? I can recall the days of living for the moment." I sighed, sliding back on the couch in a pout.

"I know McKayla is pregnant, so you can't hang out like you used to."

"That's true."

"The men are waiting. Besides, I have a proposal for you."

"Nikki, you're sweet, but I like men—tall, athletic build, wide shoulders, and sexy smile."

She giggled and clinked glasses with me.

"Not proposing to be your woman. This is a business opportunity."

"What's the business opportunity?"

"Get dressed, and we can talk about it on the way to the spa."

Nikki reached in another bag and pulled out a blue silk, ruffled cocktail dress.

"Unfortunately, I have limited funds for the spa. Can we just go to lunch?"

"My treat," Nikki said.

I pressed my lips together and narrowed my eyes.

"Where is this going?"

She wiggled her brows and smacked me on the ass.

"Get dressed!"

"We have to figure out how to get around the security patrol."

"Leave it up to me."

I watched Nikki open the door, fluff her curly blond hair, and walk up to Edwin, tapping him on the back. She whispered in his ear, and he grinned, looking back at me as I waved.

"Edwin, would you mind taking us to the spa? My friend needs a little time out of the house."

"I need to call the boss," Edwin answered.

"Tell your boss we'd appreciate it if he agreed," Nikki said.

"Sure, give me a minute," Edwin replied, turning to

walk over to the other guard. Nikki rushed back in and grabbed her purse.

"Come on! We only have a minute before he comes back."

"What about me changing?"

"These are just to throw him off. We can go through the back way out of here." Nikki waved and watched as the men talked amongst themselves.

"I should have thought of that." Nikki pushed me out of the house, and I didn't get to grab my purse or phone.

"What about my ID?"

"You'll be fine." Nikki closed my apartment door, and we quickly walked down the hall to the exit.

"Aye! Stop, Rena." My legs flew down the stairs faster than I expected, and Nikki laughed as she tried to keep up with me.

"Go! Hurry before he catches us." I made it to the exit. Nikki shut the door behind us and ran down the alley to the front.

"Shit! He has people at the front."

"We'll take an Uber."

"What about your car?"

She grabbed my arm, and we ran in the opposite direction of the guards standing at the front entrance. Nikki raised her hand out to the cab that pulled up from the corner light.

"Take us to Seasons Spa please." Nikki rambled off the address, and I shut the door right as the men came from the back alley. I waved as we drove by and knew Sante would have a fit.

"I wish McKayla was here for this." I sat up and buckled my seatbelt.

"How is she doing?"

"Almost ready to have her little boy." Nikki reached in her purse and pulled out her mirror to her makeup.

"I haven't seen her in forever."

"We should have dinner one night. How long are you here?"

"A week, and then I head out to Paris."

"You're living the life."

"That's what I wanted to talk to you about."

Ten minutes later, we arrived at the spa. Nikki pulled thirty dollars out to pay the cab driver, then shut the door, and we walked into a beautiful peaceful garden of Eden.

"I don't have a job."

"Your journalist loved that work but deep down, what was your passion?"

Fashion design was something I dreamed about growing up. Playing pretend in the mirror with different bedspreads and trying to make gowns.

"Being a designer."

"Hello, welcome to Seasons Spa."

We approached the front desk, and I watched Nikki set up facial and nail appointment for us. The place had a large water foundation in the middle of the room, a table with different photos of each spa treatment, samples, and a bar in the back corner.

"For the two of us," Nikki declared.

Clerk nodded and took out her credit card to pay.

"Just go through the back doors, and they'll take you."

After picking up a lemongrass martini, I headed back to the bathroom to change into a robe.

"Are you going to tell me what today is about?"

"We're going to get dolled up and go out to dance and celebrate."

"Celebrate what?"

"You become a fashion designer."

Her words made me spit out my drink.

"Come on, it'll be fun." Nikki waved me over to the massage table, and I lay across from her as the massage therapist took the drink from my hand and grabbed the oils. I was still trying to process her words about becoming a fashion designer. I was too old to start over, even though I didn't look it up but getting into that industry was something you needed to do early in your career, or have major connections, and I had neither.

"Stop looking worried. I have it all planned out."

LATER THAT EVENING, we went to downtown Chicago to the best dance club in town. Nikki showed me what I was missing after getting so wrapped up in my journalism career. I knew McKayla thought I was flaky sometimes and not serious about things, but not having the same nine to five was something I craved. The freedom to do what I wanted spoke to me on a deeper level after watching my mother struggle to survive. The *Fever* was known all over the city as the place to be seen and mingle with the higher elite. I sipped on the dirty martini while in the VIP section, which we didn't have to pay for because Nikki knew the owner.

"Are you having fun?" Nikki yelled in my ear.

"Yes, I appreciate you getting me out there."

A hand went up to dismiss my comment.

"To the beginning of? I haven't designed in so long."

"Maybe you've gotten a little rusty, but the talent is there." Nikki pointed at the dress I wore with a wide gold belt, partnered with a gold choker necklace. I teased my hair up with a few curls hanging down. Makeup wasn't too loud, and the maroon lipstick popped to match my nails.

"Ladies, how are we doing tonight?" I scanned up at TJ, Nikki's friend who owned the place. He was handsome if you liked the pretty boy type with crystal-blue eyes, chiseled jawline, and dimples in his cheek. The problem was that I could spot a one-night stand when I saw one, because I did it often.

"We're doing amazing, TJ. Thank you again for the section." Nikki batted her eyelashes, and I smirked as TJ openly flirted back.

"If you need anything, I mean anything, let the bottle girls know." TJ kissed the back of her hand and winked. He left and went over to the bar area, pointing at our section. We waved. It was still early as more people crowded in, and the dance floor was heavy with the melodies of Jessie J playing. I jumped up, and Nikki grasped my hand to stand, bumping my hip.

"Time to dance!" She snapped her fingers and swished her hips.

"Let's get to the dance floor." I threw an arm around her shoulder.

The crowd gathered as we moved closer to the deejay booth and watched the lights change color. The large video screen on the wall changed to another song by Ariana Grande. I laughed at Nikki as she pulled a guy to her back and grinded against him. I hadn't had a date or any sex in a few weeks because of work. I sat next to them and moved my feet from side to side, letting the rhythm engross me.

"*Look at all the ladies tonight. Show the fellas what you*

got!" the deejay shouted, mixing the playlist. Nikki turned to face the guy and whispered in his ear, and he staggered over to me and grabbed me around the waist. I extended an arm around his neck.

"Want to come back to my place?" he whispered in my ear.

"What do you have in mind?"

"Arghhh!" he groaned, dropping to the ground in pain, I glanced up, and my eyes ballooned in shock at Sante holding a gun, casting a harsh glare. I went to bend down to help the guy, and Sante glared at me.

"Move away from him now, Rena."

"What is wrong with you?!"

"Let's go."

"No! I'm here with my friend. Are you crazy." I started to help him up.

Pop! Pop!

Sante shot in the air, and the crowd screamed, running off the floor and out of the building. I jumped back in shock as the dark stare held me in place.

"Sante, calm down."

"If you touch him, I will kill him."

A shiver ran through my body.

"He's innocent."

"Take her." He motioned at his men, who I noticed were on both sides of me. I watched them grab Nikki, and the guy I was dancing with tried to stand and swing on Sante. I guess he was still dazed because he missed, and Sante punched him in the nose, then put him in a headlock.

"Try it again and see what happens." Sante gritted through his teeth, stared at me.

"Who are you? I'm calling the police." TJ ran over

toward us. Sante pointed the gun at him, causing him to freeze with his hands up.

"TJ Hutton, I'm Sante Calabresi. If you want to keep your life, you'll ignore what happened tonight," Sante said, and TJ looked at me, then Nikki.

"Calabresi Family," TJ muttered, and Sante smiled. TJ turned to walk away and shook his head at Nikki.

"TJ, wait! Call the police," I shouted and tried to wiggle out of the guard's arms.

"You can yell all you want. No one's coming, cara." Sante laughed, let the guy go, and walked up closer to me. Sante put the gun away and cupped my chin.

"I don't chase, and I'm not Savio."

"You could never be half the man Savio is. At least he cares about people."

He sighed and shook his head.

"Take her out to the car."

"I want to go home!" I yelled, and his men ignored my words. The entire place was emptied out as people jumped in their cars to leave. I tried to push the passenger side door open, but the childproof lock prevented me from escaping. I slammed my hand against the window, then my foot.

"Let me out of here!" I yelled, pounding on the door. When it opened, and Sante slid in next to me, I tried to jump over him to get out. He grasped me around the waist, gripped my wrists, and pushed me down on my back with us chest to chest, breathing hard.

"Nikki, call the police!" I hurriedly screamed. She was locked in her seat next to another guard, and I was pissed that my friend was involved with this family.

"Stop fighting, or you'll hurt yourself."

"Let me up." I felt a cry rising to my throat.

"Do you think I like running behind you to keep you safe?"

My chest rose and fell, breathing harshly.

"I need you to protect me." I huffed out a breath.

"Rena, who are these people?" Nikki probed, and I tried to bite Sante's hand.

He smiled as he raised his left brow. My skin tingled at the scent of his cologne, and I closed my eyes so that I wouldn't be distracted from the beauty of his smile.

"I'll let you go if you don't try to bite me."

I blew out a breath.

"Fine."

In response to Sante's removal of his hands, I backed up to the edge of the door.

"Nikki, I'm sorry. I never planned on you getting involved in my problems." I motioned at Sante and his guard. The limo drove out of the club's parking lot.

"I'm a friend of Rena's."

"He's McKayla's brother-in-law." His carefree attitude made me roll my eyes.

"Okay, so why did you stop us from going out tonight and the guards at her apartment?" Nikki asked, and I begged with my eyes for Sante not to reveal his family background. The number of times my life had been pranked by them was endless.

"I'm a businessman. I'm sure Rena has told you how we are very high profile and need to make sure anyone who comes in contact with McKayla is to be protected," he explained. She didn't believe it but played it off to keep the tension down. The car stopped in front of his condo building, and my eyes drew into slits.

"Why am I here?"

"Nikki, my men will make sure you get home safely.

Rena will be in contact soon." He opened the door, stepped out of it, and extended his hand to me. It was then that my mouth dropped open.

"Sante, what is this?"

"Come now."

"No, we go together. Nikki isn't leaving my side." I knew their background and how they treated strangers. Nikki was a close friend of mine, so I couldn't see myself allowing her to be hurt or worse.

"Nothing will happen to her, I promise."

We had a stare off, and Nikki nodded for me to go ahead.

"I can't leave you."

"I'll be fine. Besides, we have a lot to talk about tomorrow."

"If one piece of hair is missing from her head, you'll answer to me." I pointed at the guard, reached to hug Nikki, and slid out of the limo, smacking Sante's hand away. The door closed, and the car drove away. I prepared myself to handle Sante Calabresi once and for all for interfering in my life.

CHAPTER
SIX

SANTE

After Rena slammed the door behind me, I pressed my hand on the knob and counted down from ten to calm my temper. Savio had to deal with chasing women with McKayla; that was something I never had or would do. The second he called to inform me about her being out with her friend that day about Greco's men, things in my life shifted. Rena was the cause and sometimes, I hated to admit, the cure. I turned the knob, walked in, and saw her pacing the floor with her hands balled up into fists. I sighed, loosened my shirt, and moved in closer to the couch to temper down any frustrations before another war unleashed.

"I got a call you escaped."

"As an adult, I don't need to escape my apartment."

"Until things are clear with our enemies. you have to be protected."

"Why? I don't mean anything to you, Savio, or anyone in this family!"

Her harsh words stopped me in my tracks.

"That's what you believe?" Amusement glinted in Rena's eyes.

"I don't know what to believe anymore."

"This wasn't the ideal situation, but you have to live here now."

Her head snapped back in surprise.

"What are you talking about?"

"Some things are happening that we need to keep you safe."

"Like what?"

"I can't answer that right now."

"Wait a minute. If it pertains to my life, you better tell me now."

"That's not how this works." A flicker of irritation and impatience shone in my eyes. As I removed my jacket and stalked off to my bedroom, she trailed behind me.

"I'll call the police."

"Go ahead."

"Kidnapping is a crime." I pinned both of my hands on either side of her on the wall.

"What do you think they'll say at the police station?" In response, her eyes leapt to my lips as she made eye contact with me. I should be terrifying, or even disgusting to her, but deep down, she knew I wouldn't hurt her unless her brother didn't come through for us.

"Move." Her eyes flashed to mine.

I stepped back, unbuttoned my shirt, and pulled it off.

"Until we catch the people that tried to kill us the other day, you stay here."

"Who's after you?"

"None of your concern."

"Oh, come on! I'm not naïve, Sante. I refuse to be locked up here."

"McKayla will call you." When I unbuckled my pants, she covered her eyes, and I chortled, stepped out of them, slid off my boxers, and headed to the bathroom to turn on the shower.

"Does this have anything to do with McKayla? Is she in trouble? ` ` She stood with her back to the door.

"All will be revealed tomorrow."

I slid the door open, stepped inside, and she turned swiftly at my comment.

"Why can't you tell me now?"

Stepping under the hot steam, I dropped my head under the water to collect my thoughts.

"Tomorrow," I called out.

I picked up the towel and soap when suddenly, the lights went out, and the door slammed shut.

"Rena! Mi fai impazzire."

Thirty minutes after showering, I walked into the living room, and she was sitting on the couch, talking to someone on the phone. I reached down and snatched it out of her hand

"Sante!"

"Who is this?"

"Sante, what have you done to Rena?" McKayla fussed. I handed it back to Rena and stalked to the kitchen to grab the food my mother made for dinner tonight.

"Do you see what I'm talking about? He's insane!" she yelled, holding the phone on the table, on speaker as she removed her shoes and jewelry..

"Savio won't tell me what's going on either," McKayla declared.

"Well, you're pregnant, so that's a reason to not worry you."

"I feel bad. This is all my fault."

"No, it's Savio and his brother's fault!" she spat. I ignored her tantrum, put my plate in the microwave, and popped the bottle of Hennessy.

Ding!

"How's the baby doing? Have you started to prepare for delivery?"

"The nursery is ready, and my bag is at the door with an extra in the car," McKayla explained. Rena cut her eyes to my food, and I ignored her somber look. Mother's lasagna was the best.

"You sound tired. Once I talk with Nikki, we can have dinner before you have the baby."

"That would be great. I haven't seen her in some years."

"She thinks I should get back to designing."

My ears perked up at her statement.

"Wow! You've always been into fashion."

Rena looked at me with a sharp look. I cleared my throat.

"Tell my godson good night for me, and I will catch up soon," Rena announced, then ended the call.

She stood from the couch, pulled her hair out of the ponytail, stretched her arms out, and yawned. Then when she flipped me off, I chuckled at her rudeness. A woman like her would never last long with me. I didn't mind a strong personality, but she needed to be submissive and understand who was in charge.

"I'm going to bed."

"Try to not disappear again."

"It kills you, doesn't it." She stopped, with her back to me as I continued to eat my lasagna.

"Go to bed, Rena."

"No."

"Do as I say!" I slammed my hand on the table.

In her anger, she stomped toward me and pointed her finger at me.

"I am not your minion or girlfriend. You can't control me, Sante." I jumped up, and the chair flew back. I gripped her chin and pulled her close to my chest. My nostrils flared as her hands pushed at my chest.

"You will be whatever I tell you to be. This is my last warning." Tears stung her eyes as her lips parted. Part of me wished to be selfish and not to be selfish. She needed to realize there was too much at stake, and family must take precedence. In our bloodline, honor, code, and brotherhood predominated. I would destroy Carmine and the Colombo family whatever the cost, and if that ended up hurting her brother unless he conceded to my terms, then it was done. I released her and stepped back, picked up the chair, and sat to finish eating.

"You've changed," she voiced.

"No, I've always been this way. You've just been handled differently for McKayla's sake."

It was as if a light went on in her head, and she comprehended that the calm Sante she met before no longer stood for her disobedience.

"What do you want from me? I know it's not money; you got me fired already." While wiping a tear from her cheek, she pleaded.

"We'll talk tomorrow."

"Okay," she muttered, shifting in the direction of the guest bedroom down the hall.

Dropping the fork, I clenched my hands together in thought. Letting out a long-held breath, I stood, carried my dishes to the sink, and cut out the light. As I strolled down the hallway, I heard sniffling from the guest bedroom. As my hand reached to knock, I stopped and changed my mind. The day has been hard for everyone, and more fighting would make my next move more difficult. Turn and head around the corner to my bedroom, shut and lock the door, tread into the bathroom to brush my teeth and climb into bed.

THE NEXT MORNING, she'd given me the silent treatment, and I avoided forcing any conversation until I needed an answer. I left Marilyn with her since Elio, Renato, and I drove to our meeting. I'd arranged a meeting with Senator Ted Clark. All he knew was that a business was interested in fundraising with his likeness, and any politician who wanted publicity would run at the chance. McKayla was too close to giving birth, so Savio stayed behind, and Vincenzo held more responsibility at the main office. The SUV stopped at the private entrance, we stepped out, and Senator Clark's aide reached a hand out for me to take.

"Mr. Calabresi, we were surprised to receive your request."

"I know it can be difficult sometimes to bring light to issues."

"I'm Sheldon, Senator Clark's aide. Please follow me."

"These are my brothers Elio Jr. and Renato." They both nodded and shook his hand. Sheldon escorted us into the building, and I watched the congressmen and staff move in and out of the hall. A few members of the press hung around, recording. We went through the metal detectors without issue. I told Renato if he came, it would have to be without a gun. As long as our men stayed close by with protection, we'd be fine. Sheldon opened the door of Ted's office, and he stood talking on the phone.

"Norman, where do you think you'd be without my support?" Ted waved for us to take a seat. Sheldon went over to the coffee cart in the corner of the room, held up a cup toward us, but we declined.

Ted lowered the phone and extended his hand. "Mr. Calabresi, you have to excuse me. I wasn't expecting your call."

"Thank you for agreeing to this meeting." Renato opened his briefcase and passed me a folder.

Ted clapped his hands together and stood in front of us with his lips curved up in a devilish smile that I would wipe off his face in a minute.

"Do you mind if we talk privately?" I proposed to Ted to give us the room alone, and he directed his finger at Sheldon.

As the door closed, I opened the file and offered it to him.

"What is this?" He looked at the photos of his mother and sister in question.

"Mr. Clark, I think you should sit down."

"No, I think you should." Ted attempted to leave the room, but Renato stopped him.

"Are you crazy? Do you know who I am?" Ted shouted, and Elio locked the door.

"Please, Mr. Clark, I suggest you sit. This can be a pleasant meeting, or we could do it another way. I promise you, I'm the nice brother." I tapped the seat in front of me.

Ted walked over to his desk and sat.

"Explain why you have photos of my family?"

"You have the deciding vote on the transportation bill, correct?"

"Again, tell me why you're here."

"I'm here because you will be voting to approve the bill."

"I haven't decided."

"I've decided for you. Agree to the deal and put a provision that ACE Holdings has the exclusive distribution." I tapped on the form with our company's information.

"Ten million dollars!" Ted jumped in shock out of his seat.

"Please keep your outbursts under control."

"I'm not agreeing on this vote."

"I think you will."

"I'm calling the police." When he picked up the phone, I hit the receiver and pulled it away from his face.

"You've stolen over one million from not only your campaign funds, but you owe Colombo Cartel five million in gambling debt."

As he slumped in his chair, his hand brushed over his face.

"I can't do this; I'm already dealing with a lot."

"You will, or your family dies. From what I heard, Carmine is looking to take your sister out."

His mouth hung open in shock.

"Does she know?"

I shook my head.

"Not yet, but that can change. They've already made an attempt." I lied. Carmine was after her, but he wanted us more. This was the opportunity to use Rena's family connection to get our business locked in as a sole proprietor.

"It was a mistake."

"Gambling is never a mistake when you put your sister up as insurance."

"I've been on the news, talking about not voting."

"Tell them you changed your mind."

"I can pay you back and him."

"The house you live in is close to being sold, and the home you bought for your mother is under your charity's name."

"Rena and I haven't had the best relationship for the last few years."

"Save that for your therapist, Mr. Clark."

"How do I know you won't kill them after I agree to vote?"

"That's a risk."

"I need insurance."

"You not dying is the best insurance."

"Rena hasn't agreed to some of the ways in which I do business, but I love my sister."

"Rena wouldn't be harmed under our protection."

"What does that mean?"

"She's going to be my wife."

"Wha...t," he stuttered.

"I needed insurance as well in case you tried to renege or go to the police. Rena will become my wife, and you sign the documentation. In return, you will pay off your debts."

He looked from Renato to Elio and back to me.

"I don't know about getting your company involved."

"You're the politician. Make it happen. Sign the document."

I pulled out a pen and pressed it in his hand. I watched him sign, and he dropped his head down in his hands.

"Cheer up, you get to keep your life and job. No one has to know."

"You son of a bitch!" The moment Ted charged at me, I grasped his arm around his back and put him in a choke hold.

"Try not to get so emotional. You'll still be able to rob the public blind."

"Fuck you," he seethed, and I let him go. I grabbed the photos and documents up and passed them to Elio to put away. I straightened my coat and fixed my tie, heading to the door.

"She won't agree to this marriage."

"Let me worry about Rena. You just keep your end of the bargain, or I'll have Renato handle things his way."

We left his office and met up with Sheldon, sitting at his desk.

"How did it go? Are you onboard with the donation?" I smirked, clapping him on the back.

"He was enthusiastic about the donation. Thank you for setting it up."

"Mr. Clark is known for his charity work. This will be great for the next cycle on the campaign trail."

"Glad we could be of service."

We walked out of the building and climbed in our car. I waited for Renato and Elio to go off on me about my proposal. I didn't explain the full details, and I knew the moment I told Rena, we'd be at each other's throat.

"Before you both chew me out, I had to make a decision."

"Marriage though?" EJ voiced.

"If I knew another way, I would have."

"Am I going to be the only brother single?"

"I'm single." In response, EJ ignored Renato's comment.

"Does Cora know that?" Renato's brow rose.

A glare from EJ greeted him.

"I wanted to ask you about Cora."

"What about her?"

"You seemed uptight when she was around the day of the shooting."

"What are you implying?" EJ answered.

"Nothing."

"This won't sit right with Savio."

"I made a decision. Either you back me as the underboss, or you don't."

They eyed me to see if I gave off any sense of fear. As their older brother, I was the one who made things right whenever they'd get into an argument or fight. Many times, I'd defuse situations, but for me to step out on a limb and force a hand, it was for a reason.

"We'll let you tell him."

"I want to be there when you tell Rena," Renato joked.

"She'll take it well."

"Rena Clark taking something well?"

"A woman won't turn down a marriage in the Calabresi Family."

SEVEN

SANTE

The next day

"No way in hell!" she growled.

I ducked low to avoid a glass vase flying aside my face.

"You throw one more thing at me, I'm going to show you what I'll do."

As Renato grabbed a hold of her, she tried to wiggle free.

"Renato, let me go! You're just as fucked up as the rest of this family."

"Let me explain."

"My brother called and told me you threatened him." With rose-colored cheeks and lips pressed together, Rena spoke through gritted teeth.

Renato and I made eye contact.

"I'm going to be honest with you, Rena."

"Too late! I already knew you and this family were heartless!" In response, I tossed my chin up at Renato and let her go. While I took a deep breath, I prepared to confess the truth to Rena about her brother's lies.

"Rena, have a seat."

"I prefer to stand." Her full breasts spilled under her crossed arms.

"We're going to have an adult conversation without screaming." My mouth jerked into a grin.

"I believe you have me confused with the other bimbos."

My tongue glided over the top of my lip.

"Your brother isn't who you think he is, Rena."

"He's a straight-laced senator. I know like any other pencil pusher, they aren't perfect, and we weren't extremely close, but he's family."

"Did you know he purchased your mother's home with campaign funds?"

She stumbled back at my reveal.

"You're lying." She barely breathed the word.

"He owes Carmine of the Colombo Family over five million dollars."

"What!"

"Ted Clark is a gambler who owes a lot of people, and he's the reason your life is being turned upside down."

"No... No... that's not true." My attention was drawn to Rena's hands, which indicated that I should stop talking.

"I might be an asshole, but I don't like him, Rena."

Renato pulled out the file we had on Ted and showed her the proof of her brother's debts.

"Carmine wasn't only one putting a hit on us, but you as well."

"You're trying to turn me against my family."

"I'm trying to save your life!" I argued, and she ran a hand through her hair.

"These could be fakes." She held the photos up.

"Carmine won't touch you if we get married, and I handle the debt."

Her fingers held on to her trembling lips, biting at her bottom lip.

"Why would you do that?"

"Because we have a deal in place that would put my family in a nice position for our business."

As soon as she heard that, she laughed drily and whistled.

"Money, that's what this is all about… money."

"He has the lone vote that could place millions and open more jobs for our company."

"Please don't act like you're helping people."

"Carmine doesn't care if your brother is a senator. He'll kill you and your mother."

"Does McKayla know?" she requested.

"No."

"Savio."

I sighed and stood.

"I'm going to tell him today, along with my parents."

"A marriage of convenience."

"You'll be able to still live your life, Rena."

"My life is ruined because of you."

"It won't be for long."

"Why? Are you planning to kill me after the vows?"

Renato chuckled, and I flipped him off.

"Rena Fashions, You need seed money, right?"

"So, you'll buy my silence, so you can continue corrupting the city with your dirty money."

"Rena."

"No, Renato." Tightness gripped my chest as he approached her to sit beside her.

"Renato, I can handle it from here."

His hands were raised in surrender as he made his way to the door.

"Call me later."

A couple of minutes later, Renato left the condo.

"If I don't agree." Her words came out as a whisper.

"No choice." Her eyes followed me as I stood and reached down to grab the file from the front of her and headed to the kitchen. I grabbed two glasses and a bottle of scotch and poured a shot for both of us in celebration.

"I want a million dollars." She picked up the glass and tapped her finger on it as she contemplated something.

"You'll have it once we get married."

"I'm not sleeping with you."

I bent down in front of her with both hands on the chair, staring at her lips.

"Hate to love is a powerful thing." I stood.

"We should tell my McKayla."

"That can be arranged. What about your mom?"

"What's going to happen to her house? She's lived there for years."

"I'm going to have my men look into getting the name signed over to her after we figure out how much he owes the campaign."

"He really gambled that much money?"

"Tell me about your relationship with him."

She shrugged her shoulders and picked up her purse and phone. I opened the door for her to leave first. The guards motioned us to the elevator, and she punched the button for the door.

"We were close at one point, but he started to get more and more money hungry."

Taking the elevator down, I stepped out to my awaiting limo.

"He had some offshore accounts in your name, Rena."

Her head whipped around at my words.

"Ted wouldn't do that."

"Your brother is no better than I, if you want me to be honest, Rena."

I buckled my seatbelt, as the door closed and rode to Savio's home.

"I need to talk to him."

"Why? So he can lie or manipulate you?" An angry sneer escaped my lips.

"Whatever."

THE LIMO ARRIVED out front of Savio's mansion, and the gate opened, with the driver pulling into the front of the house. He stepped out and opened the door for Rena. I came around the other side and reached for her hand.

"We're not married yet." She smacked my hand away, and I shook my head. The door opened to Marilyn, and she hugged Rena, then me.

"She's been hoping you'd stop over. The baby can come any minute," Marilyn stated, and I closed the door behind us and kissed her cheek.

"Are you ready for a baby in the house, Marilyn?"

A dishtowel was thrown against my chest.

"The first grandchild for the family? Your mom is here now."

"Then I know I can't stay long with all you women here," I joked, and she giggled.

Rena went toward the loud laughing, and I followed.

"Is Rena all right?" Marilyn asked. As I circled her shoulder, I pulled her to my left side.

"She will be. We have some things to discuss with the family."

"This calls for your father?" Her head shifted up toward me.

"Sante dear, what are you doing here?" My mother held her arms out for a hug.

All the men towered over the women in the family.

"I came with Rena to check up on McKayla." My mother looked from Rena to me, then back at me. Her glare gave away the tension between us.

"What's going on? Rena, you've been quiet since you walked in, and I'm not used to that from you." I lowered my arm, and she stepped up next to McKayla and Rena at the stove.

"McKayla, how are you feeling?" Ignoring my mother, Rena rubbed McKayla's stomach.

After clearing my throat, I swallowed.

"Rena and I have some news."

"No, let me tell her."

"Tell us what?" Mom commanded.

"We're getting married." Rena blurted out.

Mother excitedly squeezed Rena, then me, into a hug.

"When did you two start dating?" McKayla asked, pointing between us.

"Should I tell them or you?"

"Rena."

"It's fine, Sante. My whole life has been ripped apart. My brother stole money and gambled from the Colombo Family, and that's why Carmine shot at us."

"Rena, no!" McKayla gasped in shock, trying to pull her in a hug.

"Why are you crying, McKayla?" Vincenzo stood by Savio while he stormed into the kitchen. As he pulled

McKayla from Rena, he checked her face and body for injuries.

"I'm not hurting Savio. It's Rena and Sante," McKayla voiced.

He glared at me, and I knew the monster was about to come out.

"What the hell is going on in here? You see my wife is pregnant."

"Rena and I are getting married."

"Since when?"

"I handled the deal on ACE trucking."

"How?"

"To keep her alive and out of Carmine's hands, we have to get married."

"So, you two aren't in love?" Mom asked.

Rena stared at me.

"This is business."

"When are you planning to get married?" McKayla wondered.

I shrugged, not thinking the entire deal through. The quicker we handled Ted and Carmine, then the other families would have no choice because the money was guaranteed.

"Rena, do you have an opinion about this?" Mom commanded, moving a hand to her hip.

"Honestly, I haven't had a chance to tell my mom or talk to my brother," Rena replied. If she thought her brother was coming to the wedding, that would never happen. McKayla and Rena walked off to have some privacy, and I stood with my family.

"Why am I the last one to find out about you and Rena?" Vincenzo grilled me, and I snorted at his harsh glare. I removed my phone from my pocket and scrolled to the details of the business proposal as we stayed in the room discussing the next steps.

A WEEK LATER, Rena refused to come out of her room like last time. Today, I had meetings on opening ACE and tracking Ted's movements. I didn't have Marilyn or any help with cooking like Savio had with McKayla. It made sense because the baby was coming, but cleaning and cooking was therapeutic for me. I knocked on the guestroom door, and loud music played.

Knock! Knock!

The door swung open, and my eyes scanned from her head down to her curvy frame in a bra and panty set.

"Yes." She crossed her arms, pushing her breasts up.

"I cooked breakfast." I cleared my throat, not knowing where I wanted to put my hands. Her smooth, coral hue was distracting, and I darted my tongue across my lips. I needed to remind myself that this was only business.

"I'm not hungry," she stressed, stepped back, and slammed the door in my face before I could respond.

"The food will be left in the microwave. I have to leave for work," I called out, and no response was given.

"Marriage is already becoming complicated."

I stomped over to my room and picked up my suit jacket, keys, and gun. Vincenzo told me the board wanted me to explain about this new venture in trucking. Plus, I had a meeting with Serbians about possibly purchasing from us. I opened the front door, then stopped and turned to look over my shoulder. No more coming home to a quiet and peaceful home at the end of the day or slipping out to meet a woman at a hotel. I had a wife to think about now and even though we weren't together for real, I would hurt her feelings by sleeping around on her. Stepping out, I felt my phone vibrate and saw a text from Danny saying he was downstairs waiting for me in the car.

Climbing out of the elevator, I saw building security monitoring the area. I stepped up to the front counter and placed my arms on top.

"Mr. Calabresi, how are you today?" Andy asked.

"Doing great, Andy. Are you just starting now?" I checked my watch and saw it was ten minutes to nine.

"Yes, sir. I am."

"I have a guest upstairs. My men will be monitoring twenty-four hours, but in case anything needs my attention, please contact me immediately." I removed my business card from the inside of my coat pocket and slid it over the counter to him.

"A guest, as in a woman?" He had a perplexed look on his face, and I laughed.

"My wife."

"Wife!" Surprised, he staggered backward, and I tapped the counter with my knuckles, heading to the waiting car.

"Where to today, Mr. Calabresi?" Danny asked, holding the door open.

"To the warehouse."

"Yes, sir."

He shut the door, went around to the driver's door, and climbed in. I logged into the cameras of my condo and watched to see if Rena came out of her room. Surprisingly, she was talking on the phone, wearing black tights, and a crop top with her hair pulled up in a ponytail.

Whoever she was talking to made her laugh, and that pissed me off for some reason. I left the camera app and went to the group text thread with Vincenzo and explained that I'd be a little late for the meeting with the board. When we arrived, Danny started to get out of the car, but I already had men waiting for me and didn't need him as backup.

"Stay here and keep the car running."

"You got it, boss."

I moved out of the car and fixed my jacket before sliding the phone in my pocket and shaking hands with Vlado as he put his cigarette out.

"You kept your word," he stressed.

"Of course, Vlado."

Vlado Dedich ran the largest mafia family in his country, and they wanted to expand to America. At first, we didn't want to bring in more families to the table or in the business. The money he was willing to spend for trafficking his guns would make all this worth the trouble.

"Do you have the amount you're willing to do?"

"Still confirming with my brother. As the Don of the family, he needs to sign off, but he trusts my decisions. I think one or two trucks a month."

"The amount of crates with guns."

"Three apiece."

"If we want to double?"

"Right now, I can't set it for that full amount until we've locked in the details."

"You promised we wouldn't have any problems."

"And you won't. If you want to get in this way, you have to be patient."

Vlado watched me for a few seconds, then looked back at his men. If he thought he would start some shit,

I'd be more than happy to show him why they called me a wolf. When it was time to find my target, I could sniff them out in a split second. His hand reached out, and I released mine for a shake.

"If you don't deliver?" he asked.

"I always deliver, Vlado. Don't worry." I slapped him on the back, and we laughed.

"Don't make me regret this, my brother."

"We're in this together." I chimed in and talked over more numbers. He'd have to bring in at least a million a crate to even get my brothers on board. Finally, after ten minutes of going back and forth, I shook hands again and left to get over to the office. Beating traffic, I made it an hour later and hopped off the elevator, passing my coat and briefcase to my assistant. I went to the conference room where Vincenzo was going over the latest updates. I pushed the door open and saw Savio, Elio, and Renato here today. Usually, Renato wouldn't be involved in coming to meetings, but he just wanted to hear how things went.

"Here's the man of the hour," Vincenzo said.

"Thanks for getting things started, Vin."

"Anytime," Vincenzo answered.

"Gentlemen. Renato, surprised you came in for a meeting."

"Thought I would come check out the way things are being run." He leaned his hands behind his head, relaxing in his chair.

"I assumed Vincenzo passed out the details."

"I did," Vincenzo responded, and I picked up the remote to change the screen.

"What exactly are you proposing, Sante? Calabresi Inc has investments all over the world. Why trucking?"

Albert, the longest-standing board member who used to be my father's accountant, moved up to a voting member.

"Albert, glad you asked. Import/export is the future where we are already in real estate and construction."

"Is that putting us on the government's radar?" Albert stated. I pointed an index finger at him.

"You're right, which means this deal will come at a cost, but I have a way to make it so we're the only company signed off."

"How?"

"We have a connection with a senator," Savio answered, and I grinned.

"My brother-in-law is Senator Ted Clark," I explained, changing the document to a picture of Ted talking with another senator.

"He's your brother-in-law. Since when?" Albert asked, surprised.

"Doesn't matter. He's on board with voting in our favor."

The room erupted, and I felt accomplished. I raised my hand up high to calm everyone down.

"Give me a second to explain. Ted is the hold-out vote on the transportation bill."

"He's not going to just vote in your favor. What do you have on him?" Albert suspected.

"Ted and I had a little talk."

"Is this going to fall back on the company? Your father know about this?" Albert challenged me, and I hated being checked.

"My father will agree to whatever we decide. At the end of the day, my brothers and I have fifty-one percent vote. This is a courtesy." I spoke plainly and direct. Albert could join Ted if he fucked me over.

"Sante..." Savio dryly scolded, and I nibbled on the inside of my jaw to control my temper.

"My apologies. I'll give you time to look over the proposal." I ended my meeting and watched them get up to leave the room. My brothers and I stood around the conference table in thought, and I just knew they'd have more questions on how I conducted myself with Albert.

EIGHT

RENA

The setting was perfect to be here with my mom and enjoy ourselves with drinks and food. I only wished I could be home in a normal situation and not some soon-to-be mobster's wife. I ordered food to be delivered to Sante's home.

When my phone vibrated, I swiped it off the table and saw she was downstairs. I hit the call button to allow her upstairs on the elevator. McKayla thought it would be a good idea to do this intimate setting, but Sante didn't give a choice. I wouldn't bring my mom in on the chaos that was about to happen.

"Sorry for being so vague with the address." I moved around her to allow her entrance and shut the door.

"Who lives here?" I took her coat and hung it on the rack, next to her purse on the table.

"Come sit down."

"Rena, what's going on?"

She hesitantly walked behind me, and I was nervous, even at my age of thirty.

"Lunch is here."

"Tell me now because you seem off. Does this have anything to do with that guy the other night?"

I blew out a breath.

"Sit down, Mom."

She pulled out a chair, as I grabbed the sparkling water and poured us each a small amount.

"I'm here so talk to me."

"The guy you met the other night is going to be my husband."

She held her hand up to cut me off.

"Wait, your husband?" Darla Clark had the same look when I told her I was going to travel the world instead of going straight to college. Being free and adventurous was my nature; I liked to explore and not be confined.

"How long have you known him?"

"He's McKayla's brother-in-law."

"That doesn't answer my question."

I picked up the salmon and placed it on my plate, along with salad and steamed veggies.

"A few months, a year."

"Months or a year."

"Mom, you don't have to worry."

"That means I need to worry more."

"You've never liked any of my brothers."

"Tell me the truth."

Ted and I were both in a position to get our mom hurt over the mafia issues with Carmine. Sante would love nothing more than to torture my family even more if I ran away again.

"The truth is that we've gotten closer since Savio and McKayla got together," I lied. We got closer when I was first kidnapped because I forced myself to overrun his space. I did everything to piss him off, and this time I wanted to avoid him altogether.

"I don't like this, and your brother hasn't picked up any of my calls."

I gulped the water down.

"What do you mean?"

"I tried calling him the night you left with that guy."

"Ted is a busy man, Mom."

"Still have a bad feeling about you marrying someone I haven't met very well."

"Support me, please. I'm happy." I lifted her hand to my cheek.

"Always, my baby, so I have to protect you."

"I'm a big girl now. You should worry for him." I cackled, and she smiled at my response.

"Maybe a family dinner for you, Ted, your future husband, and me."

"Uhmm...I don't think that will work with their schedules." Sante and Ted would be at each other's throat.

"If you want me to be on board, then I need to meet him, and I want your brother to meet him as well."

"Let me see what I can find out."

"Tell me what else is going on with you?"

"I'm out of work as you know. My apartment is gone, so Sante insisted I live with him."

"He seems controlling."

Sante could be controlling, but I was more than capable of handling him. People should be more worried for his safety than mine. Next time he fucked with my work again, I wouldn't hesitate to put a bullet in him and pray his brother's never found out.

"So, what are you going to do about work? Another newspaper?"

"I haven't decided yet. I have a little savings to hold me over." I hadn't told her about the million dollars I would get from Sante once we got married.

"Let me know if you need anything."

I bent over, circled my arm around her chair, and pulled her in close for a hug.

"Love you, Rena."

"I love you more and appreciate you not hounding my decisions."

"I was young once, I understand."

"McKayla's having a boy."

"When are you going to give me a grandchild?"

I shivered in my seat.

"No babies for me."

"Does Sante know that?"

"No."

"That's something you should talk about before getting married."

She didn't have to worry about confusion on children, I would never sleep with Sante so children weren't a factor. He could have his women, and I'd have my friends on the side. We would be married in name only.

"Believe me, he doesn't want kids either."

LATER THAT AFTERNOON, after lunch with my mom, I had one of Sante's bodyguards drive me over to McKayla's house. When we had to stop at a gas station to refill, I opened the door to step out, but he blocked me from leaving.

"Mrs. Calabresi, you have to stay in the car."

"What's your name?"

"Viktor, ma'am."

"Viktor, call me Rena. I'm not married yet or old."

"Mr. Calabresi wants us to be professional at all times."

"He's not here, is he?

"No, ma'am. I mean, sorry, Rena."

He smiled, and I winked a left brow.

"It's a gas station; no one's going to do anything here. Besides, I want to grab some snacks and use the restroom."

Viktor looked nervous, and I felt bad about the stress of my running away with the other guards, so I promised Sante I would behave this time.

"Look, I left my wallet and phone in the car. I can't run off. Just give me five minutes."

"Five minutes," Viktor said.

"Great. Do you want anything?" I started to head in the direction of the store.

"No." He pulled out the gasket and inserted his credit card in the machine to pay. Upon entering the store, I went straight to the candy aisle, grabbed a chocolate bar, and scanned the top shelf for chips. Pringles were McKayla's favorite snack, so I grabbed them, turned, and bumped into a hard chest. I nearly dropped my items, but he caught them.

"Sorry about that," I said, smiling up at him.

The faded smile on his face vanished and returned a hard stare to me. Then he stepped closer, and I backed up.

"Rena, right?" He reached up and twisted his finger in my hair.

"Who are you?"

"Name's Carmine."

My eyes grew wide in nervousness.

"Where's Sante?"

"I... I... don't know," I stuttered, trying to move around him. I was caught between the bathroom and the coffee section.

"He owes me."

"Maybe I can call him."

He moved one of my hair strands behind my ear.

"Please don't touch me."

"What are you going to do if I don't?" he hissed, slamming the food out of my hands.

"Arghh!" I gasped. He yanked me toward him by my wrist.

"He did pick a looker." He pressed a finger to my cheek.

"Please move away from me, or I'll scream."

"Rena!" Viktor yelled, and the Carmine guy smirked, ran off to the opposite end of the store, and out the back. Viktor came over to me, and I felt a little more relaxed.

"What's taking so long?"

"Huh?"

"We need to get going. Sante likes to keep you on a schedule."

"I'm almost ready. Just need to pick up a few more things." Since Sante was already dealing with Carmine and with the shootout, I didn't want to add more trouble to Sante's life. Then Victor helped me grab ice cream and Twizzlers. I reached into my pocket to pull out money to pay, but he stopped me.

"Mr. Calabresi doesn't want you paying for anything."

Viktor passed the credit card to the cashier. She

bagged everything up, and I thanked her as we walked out of the store. Out of curiosity, I glanced back at the exit door near the employee area again. He was Carmine, the man responsible for my attempted murder.

Viktor helped me in the car, and I looked around the gas station for any cars that he rode in to get his license plate, but nothing stood out. I stared out the window as Viktor played music on the radio.

Buzz!

When I looked at my phone, I saw McKayla's name flash across and chuckled. As she got farther along, she got more impatient.

"Hello, soon-to-be mommy."

"How far away are you?"

"Not that far. Why?"

"Did you get my Pringles?"

I rolled my eyes, even though she couldn't see me. She was quick to change the subject to food almost every five minutes.

"Yes, I got your Pringles."

"Savio's trying to hide all my junk food."

"He's looking out for you."

"He's a bigger asshole now that I'm pregnant."

The car pulled up to their gated property.

"The car is pulling in the driveway now."

"Perfect, hurry up." She ended the call, and I chuckled at her impatience.

Viktor parked, turned the car off, started to get out, but I stopped him.

"You can take the rest of the day off, Viktor."

"Sante wants us with you all day, Rena."

"You follow rules, huh?"

"Yes, ma'am."

"Boring." I slammed the car door after me and held the bags in my hand as the door opened to Marilyn.

"Marilyn, how are you?" We hugged at the door before she shut it behind me.

"Good, Rena. Did you get her favorite Pringles?" Marilyn asked, and I nodded.

"Yes, where's the gritty woman at?"

"In here!" McKayla yelled from upstairs.

"She's in the bedroom lying down."

"Is she all right?"

With my bags in hand, I headed to the stairs while Marilyn veered toward the kitchen.

"Savio fussed her again about cookie crumbles in the bed." Marilyn giggled, and I laughed.

"She's pregnant. He has to get used to that."

"Cheer her up."

"Where's Savio?" I stood at the top of the stairs.

"At his parents!" she yelled from the entrance of the kitchen. When I turned and opened the door of the bedroom, I saw McKayla laid out on the bed with a back pillow behind her, surrounded by her computer and papers.

"What are you doing?"

"Working."

"You're on maternity leave." I closed the computer and moved it to the vanity dresser.

"Shhhhh... Don't tell Savio."

"I need to talk."

"What's wrong?"

I passed the bag of chips and ice cream to her, as I picked up a chocolate bar.

"You can't tell Savio or anyone else."

"Tell me."

"I saw Carmine."

"Who?"

"Carmine, the one who arranged for us to get shot outside the Calabresi building."

"Where did you see him?" She tore off the top of the Pringles can and popped a chip in her mouth.

"At the store, a few minutes ago."

"Did he threaten you?"

"Kind of." I reached in the can of chips.

"Kind of, Rena."

I handed her a piece of the chocolate bar.

"I'm just wondering if Sante is telling me everything."

"Like?" She winced, then raised her hand to her stomach.

"The baby is kicking."

"Yep, I can barely sleep some nights."

"I don't know, but I'm going to talk to Ted."

"When's the last time you talked to him?"

"Months, probably a year or so. He has this idea of what I should do with my life."

"When you get into public life, it changes people."

"He was like this even before he became a senator. We used to be close, but things changed." I reached for the remote and changed the channel to the movie section.

"Maybe leave this in Sante's hands. What about a job?"

"He's the reason I don't have a job or did you forget."

"Samira won't hire you back?"

"No, and I'm not sure I want to go back anyway."

"Think it through before you go to Ted. You know how Sante can get if you get involved. Same as Savio, they blow a lid if something happens to their women."

"I'm not his woman, McKayla," I groaned, rubbing a hand down my face.

"Have you told him about children?"

"You're the second person to bring that up."

"Who else?"

"My mom."

She sat up against the headboard higher.

"How was lunch with her?"

"It was fine. She wanted to know more about Sante and thinks the wedding is a mistake."

"Children were never your priority, so this is going to be interesting."

"We can't stand each other, so having sex won't be an issue."

She pursed her lips into a thin line and cocked her head to the left.

"What?"

"The chemistry between you two is steaming. Give it time."

"I have no desire to sleep with Sante, nor does he want to sleep with me."

McKayla laughed, and I think threw a chip at her, caused her to laugh more. Then I felt the bed get warmer.

"Oh my God! I just peed my pants." McKayla cackled, I jumped out of the bed.

"You just peed all over the bed. Savio is going to kill you."

"Sshhh... help me up."

I shook my head, went to the right side of the bed, moved her legs to face me, and grabbed her hand so she could stand.

"Pull the sheets off and let me go shower. Marilyn can throw them in the washing machine."

"I'm telling Savio you wet the bed."

"You better not." She wiggled a finger at me.

"We'll see."

"Then I'll tell Sante you're in love with him." McKayla stood at the bathroom door, leaving me speechless.

"You're a mean pregnant woman."

"Promise something."

"What?"

"Leave Carmine and Ted alone." I heard her turn the shower on in the bathroom.

"McKayla...." I whined, throwing my hands in the air.

"Serious, Rena, you're my child's godmother, and we've been through a lot."

"I promise," I mumbled to myself.

"What?"

"I said I promise!" I shouted, tossing the sheets to the floor.

A *week later*

The only way I could get away without a major issue was to bring Viktor with me and tell him I was visiting McKayla. I got my brother to meet me for lunch for the first time in a while, and a part of me felt like that little girl when her father walked out on his family. Viktor was parked out front in a limo, watching the restaurant, and I had a private section reserved so we wouldn't be disturbed. After I left McKayla's home that day, I contemplated what she said but felt like I was making the right decision for me and my family.

"Rena."

I peered up at the voice which didn't match the man I remembered growing up with. He looked almost like a different person than the stocky kid I knew, with short, blond curls, who was always stuck in his room, playing video games and not letting me play.

"Ted, wow! You look...Wow." I stood and snaked my arm around his back, giving him a hug. He was taller than I remembered.

"Same to you." As he removed his shades, I noticed the bodyguards standing at the next table over.

"Do you ever get tired of the guards?" I pointed at them, declining the menus from the waitress.

He looked over his shoulder and laughed.

"A part of the job now."

"I guess it is." I fumbled with the fork on the table.

"So, why'd you request to meet?"

Upon approaching our table, the waitress greeted us.

"Hi, here's the menu for today. My name is Olivia, and I'll be your server." Her bubbly personality reminded me of McKayla and another close friend Nikki.

"Can I get a cup of tea, a muffin, and fruit?" I murmured.

Olivia wrote on her notepad.

"Anything for you, sir?"

"Coffee is fine," Ted told her.

"Coming right up." Olivia grabbed the menus and left our table

"We haven't stayed in touch, and Momma was worried."

"I bought her a house and sent presents for her birthday every year."

"Ted, you sound ridiculous, like you didn't grow up with us."

A hand went up to cut me off.

He leaned over the table and whispered harshly, "Rena, I don't know what you expect me to say. I've been busy."

"I expect my brother to reach out when he's in trouble," I hissed, slowly.

Ted scanned the room as if someone had overheard us.

"Keep your voice down."

"No, I want to know what's going on."

"Nothing is going on. Whatever you've heard is gossip."

"Gambling, Ted."

"My private life is that… private. You can't listen to gossip."

"Well, your private life has spilled over to me and soon our mother."

"What are you talking about?"

I looked over his shoulder, then back to him.

"Carmine."

"Who's that?"

"Don't play stupid with me, Ted."

"You've obviously been at that newspaper too long."

"My job has nothing to do with this, but your gambling has put my life in danger." Olivia came back, holding our tray with our drinks and food.

"Tea, muffin, and fruit for you. Coffee for you, sir," Olivia stated, and we thanked her.

I dipped a teaspoon of sugar in my tea and cut into the muffin to take a bite.

"You have no idea what I have to put up with on a daily basis."

"Tell me, because from where I'm sitting, it doesn't compare to my life right now," I fussed, stirring the sugar in the tea.

"What is this really about? Do you need money? Is that it?" I dropped the knife on the table. "You're still living in that shitty apartment with that lousy job and want me to foot your bill."

"What?"

"Just because I made a name for myself, you want to ride my coattails."

"You've lost your mind. I want the brother who was there for me when I got scared to sleep at night from the Halloween movie."

"He grew up."

"And made some terrible decisions."

"The point you're making."

I clasped my hands together, leaning over the table.

"You fucked up, and now I'm on the chopping block with Carmine and Sante."

He spilled the coffee he was drinking onto his lap.

"Chopping block how?" he murmured to me.

"Your debts are costing me and possibly Mom's life if you don't give them what they want."

"Rena, calm down." He gripped my arm.

"No, let me go!" I snatched my arm away from him.

"Rena!"

"You touch her again, I'll have a bullet in your head before Carmine can find you." His raspy voice startled me. Taking a deep breath, I swallowed the lump in my throat.

Ted squinted in confusion, looking between Sante and me.

"You're on his side?" Ted motioned at Sante.

"I suggest you tell your men to stand down, or we'll have bloodshed in here today," Sante quipped. Ted looked behind him, and five of Sante's men surrounded Ted's guards. The place quickly quieted with no other guests around.

"Unlike Ted, I don't take sides of who's paying me more." I jabbed at the rumors of him being paid off by corporations to vote in their favor. When he talked to us about a possible congressional run, we supported him because he talked a great game about helping people.

"Time to go, Rena," Sante said, and I didn't know what made him think he was the boss of me.

"We're not finished," I said, sipping my tea.

"She's still got the same attitude from back then."

Sante grabbed Ted around the collar and threw him against the wall.

"Sante!" I shouted, watching his men try to break through to stop him from hurting Ted.

"Shut your fucking mouth," Sante harshly told him through gritted teeth.

"Let him go, Sante." I placed a hand on his arm. He looked down at me and softened at my touch. Eventually, he let Ted go after five minutes, and I felt relieved he'd listened to me without an issue.

"We need to go." Sante reached for my purse off the table. I started to say something, but he glared at me.

"Stay away from her." Sante shoved Ted against the wall and poked him in the chest.

"That's my sister!" Ted shouted to our backs.

Sante flipped him off, as we stumbled out of the coffee shop. A host of photographers surrounded us, and I covered my eyes from the flashes. Sante directed me to his car.

"You can't keep me away from my family."

"Did I say that?" Sante barked back.

Sante sat to my left in the limousine when my head whipped toward his tone.

"He's my brother, and if you think I'm going to block my family out and be under your control in this marriage, that will never happen."

"Our marriage isn't real."

His words stung, but I caught myself before he could see my startled expression.

"Good, because I'd never put up with the bullshit you do."

I pushed my purse down on the seat and crossed my arms over my chest.

"Why did you meet with Ted?"

"Why are you following me? Where is Viktor?" I just realized we were in his limo and not mine.

"I tracked your phone and called Viktor."

"You tracked my phone? Are you crazy?"

"There's someone trying to kill you or have you forgotten."

"You remind me plenty. What did you do to Viktor?"

"None of your business."

"If you hurt him, Sante..."

"Are you trying to tell me what to do with my business?"

I dropped my hands to my sides, then poked my index finger in his chest.

"Viktor did nothing wrong, and my family business is mine."

"You lied to him and tried to save him. Wish you had the courage to do this with your own brother." When I reached out to slap him, he grabbed my hand and pulled me to his chest in laughter. The tension in both of our chests heaved up and down, but to our surprise, we couldn't pull away from each other. Even though we'd been in each other's company plenty of times, this time was different. Sante pushed back a small piece of hair on my cheek. My lips parted slowly, and my eyes followed the line between his, down to the small gray hair growing in his beard.

"Am I really worth all this trouble?" I whispered, feeling his arms move down my back, squeezing my hip. Normally, a red flag in my head would warn me to stop. However, I continued to lean in as our lips barely touched, but I felt the pause in his breath.

"We'll find out." He captured my lips, snaked his tongue around mine, and I moaned and pressed my hands on his chest.

"Mmmmm..." Whimpering, he ran his hands over my plump backside and pressed me deep into his embrace. The car stopped and brought me out of my trance. I moved out of his arms and back to my seat.

"We... Ummm."

"It was a kiss, nothing more," I responded, fiddling with my bracelet on my wrist. When door opened, I got out, and he followed to his condo.

After we entered, I went straight to my bedroom and removed my coat and purse. In the mirror, I looked at my face, let my hair down, and removed my jewelry. McKayla's comment about kids just came to mind. We needed to make things clear about how we would proceed with this fake marriage. I came out of the bedroom and went to find Sante in the kitchen, but he wasn't there. I heard a conversation from down the hall and stopped at his bedroom door and knocked.

"Yeah." He opened the door, and I saw him without a shirt.

"Uhm, can I talk to you?"

"Can it wait?"

"No, it's really important."

He scanned over my appearance.

"Let me call you back, Elio."

I went back to the kitchen and grabbed up a bottle of

water from the fridge. Popping the top off, I gulped it in two sittings and waited for him to arrive. A second later, he walked off in only sweatpants with his muscles flexing, and that nonchalant arrogance wafted in the air.

"What did you want to talk about?"

I cleared my throat, tossed the empty bottle in the trash, and leaned against the counter to compose my thoughts.

"Rena, I have work to do."

"Sorry, uhm... Besides the money, I want to make sure we're aligned about things."

"What else did we forget?"

"Kids... I mean I don't want kids ever."

A shocked expression crossed his face.

"You never want children or just with me?"

"Nothing to do with you, I just like traveling and being able to go places without being tied down."

"You thought I would pressure you into kids."

I stepped away from the counter and sauntered toward him.

"I was talking to McKayla, and she reminded me that I should talk with you."

"She's right."

"You don't want kids, do you?"

"Hadn't considered the possibility."

"After you get what you want from Ted and Carmine, we'll go our separate ways."

"Is that what you want?"

The thought of never seeing him again, I couldn't express if I was sad or happy. The entire family came into my life suddenly, and now I'd be married and wondered what was expected as a wife.

"What are the duties of a Calabresi wife?" I changed

the subject, turned, and went back to the kitchen. Groceries were in the fridge, and I'd planned to make a quick salad for tonight and then try to go to the club to see my favorite band perform.

"No duties, just be loyal."

"Your mom is like the backbone of the family, right?"

"Plus my father. Everything runs through them."

"Do you want some?"

"What are you making?"

"A salad."

"No, I have dinner plans."

I dropped the spoon at his comment.

"What, a date?" I whipped around to stare at him.

"If it is?"

I shrugged my shoulders.

"Sante, you kissed me in the car and went on a date right after with another woman."

"You kissed me if I recall what happened."

"That's a lie. Your lips fell on mine." I waved the spoon at him, and suddenly, I felt his presence behind me. He spread both arms out on either side of the counter to lean his chest to my back, wrapped his hand with mine on the knife and the left hand on the tomato.

"The way you slipped your tongue in my mouth, sucked on my bottom lip tells a different story." He pressed his erection on my back.

"Sante..." I gasped and released the spoon, but he still held on.

"Concentrate."

"I... I'm fine."

I heard him chuckle behind me.

"Doesn't seem like you're fine."

"You're being an ass again."

"All I did was state the obvious."

"Which is..." I muttered, fidgeting with the cucumber.

"If you want me, just say that, Rena."

He bit the corner of my neck gently.

"Is sex required?" I blurted out, and he released his hands from the food, moved them up to my shoulder, and gave me a massage.

"What do you think?"

"Your contract."

"I would never make you do anything you didn't want to do."

"Glad to hear that."

"Viktor is fine."

"Really?" I dropped the spoon and cucumber and turned around to face him.

"Yeah, I'm not Savio. I do have some nice qualities."

I lifted my arm around his neck and pecked him on the lips.

"Thank you. He's been a great friend."

"That doesn't mean to keep things from me. He's your protection."

"I get it. Can I go out tonight?"

"No."

"Sante, we made progress, why mess that up."

"I have work early tomorrow and can't watch you. I doubt you'd stay put wherever you go."

"That's not fair."

"Life as a wife to a Calabresi."

He smirked and headed out of the kitchen. I popped a piece of the tomato in my mouth and shook my head in frustration. The biggest asshole of them all.

CHAPTER

TEN

SANTE

Early morning came, and I showered, cooked breakfast, and made it down to the office with my brothers to watch the vote. Rena didn't pout too bad last night when I told her she couldn't go out and decided to watch a movie. Once I finished my work, I stayed up to catch one of her favorites, *The Godfather*. I lied to her slightly about Viktor. I didn't fire him but had a few words and fists to his face for letting her meet with him. Ted was manipulative and only out for himself. Rena didn't need to be around him to learn any truth. He would throw her under the bus to Carmine to save himself in a second.

"They're starting." Vincenzo lifted the remote, increased the volume on the TV.

Renato, Vincenzo, and I were here to monitor that Ted completed his part of the deal. Savio and McKayla had a doctor's appointment, and Elio handled the main details with our lawyer in his office.

"He's looking smug." Renato stood from the table, grilling the screen.

"Ted wouldn't do anything stupid. We know too much."

Both looked over at me.

"*Can we have everyone please take their seats?*" the speaker said into the mic.

Buzz!

I sat up in my chair, unlocked the messages, and saw that Rena had sent photos of some wedding dresses.

"Are you watching this?" Renato scoffed, pointing at the screen.

"No." Ted sent down a vote. The room went silent, and the speaker picked up the gavel to get order in the room.

"He's fucking with us." Renato slammed his hand on the table.

"What do we do?" Vincenzo asked, and I held my hand out to calm him down.

"Hold up."

"Hold on, this bastard is playing you, Sante," Renato argued, and I couldn't disagree, but something else was going on with Ted, and I needed to find out.

"Give me a second to think."

Ted walked up to the mic, and I leaned forward on the table and ignored Rena's question altogether.

"*I need more time to look over the bill, Speaker,*" Ted commented, and I gnawed on my jaw.

"He needs to die," Renato quipped, and I agreed, but let Carmine take care of him first.

"The board members won't like the interruption," Vincenzo stated. I tapped a finger on top of the phone.

"I'll go see him."

"I'm going with you this time."

"Renato, you need to stay here."

Renato waved me off and pulled his gun out to check the chamber.

"No killing until we get the vote."

"Rather we paid someone else to vote in our favor," Renato barked back.

"This is easier. Besides, he can't run from us."

"Where does his mother live?" Renato insisted, and I promised Rena no harm would come to her mother.

"Leave her out of this."

"Not for long if he fucks us over again." Renato bumped my shoulder and walked out of the room. I trailed behind him to the elevator.

A few hours later, we arrived at Ted's office to talk and we heard chatter and excitement from the hallway to his office. A few reporters recorded the staff discussing the matter and praising him. I bypassed security and went straight to his door and knocked.

"Come in!" he called out.

I pushed it open and saw the cameraman remove the microphone from his tie, and I grew even more heated.

"We need to talk."

"Mr. Calabresi, he's in the middle of something right now," Sheldon said and I slid my hands in my pocket and stared straight at Ted.

"It's all right, Sheldon. Take the crew out and get some shots of our new proposal."

"Yes, Mr. Clark."

Everyone walked out of the room, and Renato locked the door. Ted started to stand up from the chair, and I marched around the desk and gripped him around the collar.

"Motherfucker, who do you think you are!"

"Get him off me!" Ted shouted, trying to pull my hands away.

"He's the nice one actually." Renato chuckled. I slammed Ted's face forward on the desk and removed my gun.

"Are you ready to die, Ted? Huh... tell me," I seethed, with spit flying out.

"Please, I'm sorry. I can fix everything."

Knock! Knock!

"Mr. Clark, are you all right?" Corinne, his secretary, spoke through the door.

"Tell her you're fine!" I squeezed him tighter around the neck.

"Everything's fine, Corinne," he stated calmly once I removed my hand and sat him up.

"Now I want you to set up the vote again, and you're going to end this now."

"It takes time to get that going."

I tapped the gun on his cheek.

"Rethink that statement."

"Okay, okay... I'll get them to redo the vote."

"If I have to come back down here, there's going to be a problem."

"I understand."

"Do you think Carmine is going to let you off the hook?"

"Does my sister know you're down here?"

The moment he brought up his sister, I had an itch to put a bullet through his skull.

"Rena is no longer your concern." I placed the gun

back in my holster and buttoned up my jacket, before heading out of his office.

"She won't love you!" Ted yelled. I stopped and turned to face him.

"You should worry if you'll live long enough to see her get married."

The glee dropped from his face. When Renato unlocked the door, Corinne stood from her desk, and I nodded at her.

"He's ready to see you now, Corinne."

As she slowly walked into his office, Renato and I watched them together, and I had a feeling deep down she could be a problem.

RENATO SLAMMED the door to our father's home, and he marched toward his office, as I trailed along, frustrated that Vincenzo texted the board, wanting updates.

"Did you see the vote?" Renato spoke to him.

He pulled out a cigar from the hidden spot in his desk and waved us to sit.

"I suspected he wouldn't go quiet."

"You think he's talking to the police."

"Tulio says you're on their radar at the FBI."

Renato sat up straight at his comment.

"We need to kill him," Renato snarled, nose flared.

"Renato, calm down."

"Father, that fucker is using this to get what he wants."

"Which is what?"

"Airtime, possibly a run for president."

"He doesn't have the bandwidth."

"We should get a meeting with Alize and Tommaso ASAP."

"That's good. Call Carmine."

"No."

"I'm not asking, Sante. Do it because the moment he's not aware, more bloodshed happens."

"When?"

"As soon as possible."

"I'm supposed to marry Rena in a week."

"Then you need to marry her now. If he knew she was locked under our authority, it could be better for us," Father answered.

"Okay."

"She's not going to like it, or Mother," Renato brought up.

"Women like to be swept off their feet," Father explained.

"How do you know what she likes?" I insisted and stood.

"Jealousy is showing. No one wants her but you," Renato taunted and threw his hands up.

"Hush, Renato," Father demanded.

"Who's all going to the wedding?"

"Just us."

"You're not inviting McKayla, her best friend?" Renato pried.

"Renato is right. You should have her there, Sante."

I groaned and ran a hand on top of my head.

"Can Madre put something together quickly?"

"She and Marilyn can put something here in the backyard."

"Great. I'll talk to Rena about it tonight."

"First, get the meeting with Alize."

I dialed Alize's number and put it on speaker as it ran twice before it was picked up.

"Sante."

"Brambilla."

"What's the point of your call?"

"I need a meeting with you and the other bosses."

"Is Savio going to be there?"

I glanced up at my father, and he shook his head.

"I'm leading the meeting."

"Can I ask the details?"

"Not over the phone."

"Make this the last time you call a meeting, Sante, without Savio's presence."

"I have his backing on any discussions, Alize. Keep that in your memory." I hung up and tapped the phone to my chin.

"Sounded like he's not a fan of your brother," Renato blurted out. I sighed and jumped out of the seat.

"As of now, we need his commitment, but if he doesn't align..."

Renato and I looked at my father for confirmation.

"You do what is needed, son."

"Thank you, Father."

When we left his office, we heard laughter from the front door and spotted Marilyn and my mother drinking.

"Boys, what are you doing here?" She sipped on her martini.

"Kind of early for drinking?"

"We're adults and taking a break before McKayla is done."

"Have you been to see her and Savio?"

"Yes, the doctor said it is almost time," Mom informed me.

"We'll call and check in on him."

"He'd love that," Marilyn responded.

"Besides that, I need a favor."

"How can we help our son?"

"Rena and I need to get married immediately."

"Why?"

"Things changed."

"Does she know?"

"Not yet."

"We had a schedule to go look at dresses tomorrow."

"She didn't tell me about that."

"Probably wanted to surprise you."

"Then I need to talk with her now."

I lifted my cell and dialed Rena's number.

"I'm busy, Sante." She sounded out of breath.

"Doing what?"

"Busy."

"Rena, what are you doing?"

"Working out, if that's okay."

"Yes, Mrs. Calabresi."

"What are you calling me about?"

"We have to push up the wedding."

"Why?"

"Nothing for you to worry about."

"I wanted to wait until McKayla had the baby."

"This can't wait."

"You've really fucked up my life, Sante, and it's not fair!"

"Your money will be deposited in your account as soon as we are married."

"It needs to be there now."

"Soon as we hang up."

"Fine. I'll look for a dress."

"Thank you for being cooperative."

"Just get me my money." She ended the call, and I didn't know if I wanted to ring her neck or suck on her lips as she moaned my name.

"That smile on your face tells me you're into her."

"Mother, this is business."

"Mother knows the look of a man who's interested in a woman."

ELEVEN

RENA

The next day

Sante's demand that we have the wedding immediately forced my plans to change. Now, I was here at the dress shop with McKayla on FaceTime to help pick out something. Savio put his foot down and said she couldn't leave the house now that she was close to giving birth, and I understood. So sadly, the experience of having my friend with me was cut short, but Adelina and Cora came with me since my mom refused to come. She still wanted to meet Sante on a formal level, and I hadn't had the heart to tell him just yet.

"What about this dress, McKayla?" Cora held the phone up as I stood on the podium. She moved it from the top of my head to my feet for a full view.

"I'd think you would have some lace or a long train. Maybe a mermaid dress"

"I thought of something long and silky."

"A plunging neckline."

The seamstress handed another dress to me with a plunging neckline and train.

"How about this?" I held up in front of me.

"That would be beautiful on you."

"Let me try it on, and still need to figure out the location."

"The wedding's at our home. We can get a company to come out to decorate."

"You don't need to do that, Adelina."

"You're my daughter in law and I want your day to be special."

"Thank you, but I never expected to be getting married, let alone to your son."

"He's crazy about you."

"Sante."

"Yes, you might think he's only doing this for the contract, but I see it in his eyes."

"See what?"

"He loves you."

I wouldn't want to get into an argument, but this was a business arrangement. He'd never looked at me seriously since I met him.

"What are you doing about work, Rena?" Cora pressed. I stepped off the podium, took the dress to the back, and changed.

"I was thinking of doing a fashion blog or something!"

"Fashion."

Only person who knew about my love of clothes, besides Nikki, was McKayla, who'd kept it under wraps for years. The love of designing and styling brought me happiness beyond the work I did as a writer at the new station.

"Yep, I used to design my own clothes growing up." I

stepped out of the room wearing the gown and pulled the front up to adjust my breasts.

"I think that's the one," Adelina stated, and I smiled.

I twirled in the mirror.

"You think so?"

"You look beautiful, Rena," Cora responded, clapping her hands.

"What do you think, McKayla?" I held out my hands.

"My best friend is getting married."

"Please don't start crying."

"Only happy tears."

"Well, glad it's happy-" I stopped when suddenly, McKayla's face scrunched up in pain.

"McKayla, are you all right?"

"I think my water just broke."

"Where's Savio?"

"He went to some meeting about a real estate company." McKayla breathed slowly.

"Okay, who else is with you?"

I picked up the dress and took the phone out of Cora's hand. I noticed Adelina on the other line talking to her husband.

"The guards. My parents went on vacation." McKayla groaned, rubbing her stomach.

"Call 911, and I'm on my way. Send me the name of the hospital." I ran in to get out of the dress and change my clothes. McKayla hung up, and I dialed Sante's number.

"Rena, I'm a little busy."

"Sante, it's McKayla!" I blurted out.

"What's wrong with her?"

"She's having the baby."

"Shit! All right, Savio didn't call us."

"He's not with her."

"What do you mean?"

"She said he had some real estate thing he had to do."

"I'll get him on the phone. We're on our way."

"Okay, I'm leaving the dress shop now."

"A wedding dress?"

"Yes."

"I'll see you soon."

I shook off the conversation about the dress and grabbed my bag to run out and catch up with Adelina and Cora.

"Sante's going to get in touch with Savio." I slammed the door of the limo.

"Great, Marilyn is heading back over to McKayla's now," Adelina commented, and I felt a little better that someone would get to her faster.

Forty minutes later, we rushed into the hospital and saw Renato, EJ, his father, and Sante all standing around.

"Here's Savio?" his mother asked.

"He's with her now." Sante answered and watched me with a weird look on his face.

"Are you all right?"

"Yeah, why wouldn't I be?"

"You seem nicer right now."

"I'm about to be an uncle, the best way to be."

"What room are they in?"

"I can take you."

"You don't have to."

He reached for my hand.

"Rena, relax."

"Once you come back, I want to see her. I know her mother's not here," Adelina announced.

"Sure." I let Sante continue holding my hand, as we walked through the patient area and turned to the delivery ward. He pushed the door open, and I smiled, trailing him to see McKayla hooked up to monitors and laughing with Savio.

"You look so beautiful, McKayla."

"Rena, you made it!"

I bent down to give her a hug and wiped the tears from her eyes.

"How are you feeling?"

"Better now that you're here, and Savio made it on time."

"What are the doctors saying?"

"Could be any minute or hours from now."

"Glad we had you on the phone earlier."

I placed my bag on the chair next to her bed.

"True, otherwise I would have gone crazy."

"Savio, are you doing good?"

"Ready for her to not be in pain." Savio sat at the end of her bed.

"He's going to be here soon."

"Did you pick a name?"

McKayla and Savio connected.

"Savio Jr.," he responded, and Sante shook hands with him in excitement.

The door opened, and the doctor headed in with a nurse behind.

"How are mom and baby doing?' The doctor smiled, holding her chart in his hand. The nurse checked the monitor and then her vitals.

"Do you think she's going to give birth today?" Savio asked.

Doctor checked his watch.

"She came in at five centimeters."

"Stop worrying, Savio." McKayla pouted, pulling Savio by the hand to sit near her on the bed.

"Don't worry, Mr. Calabresi. She's coming along right on time."

"Can she eat anything?" Savio pressed on.

"Savio, let them do their jobs." Adelina motioned, and the doctor chuckled.

"All dads act this way. No worry," the doctor explained as he put her blanket down after checking her.

"We'll be in the waiting room," Sante told me, and I hugged McKayla again and left to sit in the hallway.

"They'll be here all night. You two should go home," Adelina insisted.

"If something goes wrong, I'll never forgive myself."

"Nothing is going wrong. Try to get some sleep. We have a wedding to plan," Adelina responded, and we embraced again.

"Are you leaving?"

"Yeah, my brothers and I will come back when the baby is born."

"I found a dress today." I looked up at him.

"That's good. Listen, Rena..."

Before he could get a word out, his brother walked up to us.

"Sante, we need to talk," Renato interrupted.

"What's going on?"

"He voted."

Sante grinned, and that piqued my curiosity

"Who voted?"

"Ted."

"Oh… So the deal is done."

"The first part. We still need to get married."

"You still have a chance to get out of this shame of a marriage," I joked.

"I need to go handle something. Will you be good at getting home by yourself?"

"If Viktor's out there, I'll be fine."

"He's just the driver, Rena." Sante groaned, and I smirked, knowing I could get under his skin. He pecked me on the cheek and walked off with his brother. An hour later, I was home in the tub, listening to Adele and thinking over my life. I closed my eyes and remembered the many men I'd dated over the years. Ending up with a mafia boss wasn't the choice I expected to see at the end of the aisle.

Ring!

I lifted my phone and saw McKayla's name scrolled across.

"How are you?"

"He's here."

"I'm so happy for you, McKayla."

"Thanks. Savio has him spoiled already."

"It's expected for a father and son."

"That's true."

"Get some rest. I'll come see you soon."

"No, I'll be out of the hospital soon. Come by the house."

"Are you sure?"

"Positively, your godson is sleeping now. Let me get some rest."

"McKayla."

"Uh huh."

"I'm getting married."

"I know."

"I regret sometimes going to the club that night."

"A part of me should say the same, but I wouldn't have my son right now."

"True, love will have you reflecting I guess."

"Are you in love with Sante, Rena?"

Clack!

I heard a door shut, and I wondered if Sante heard McKayla's question.

"Good night, McKayla."

"You have to answer that one day."

"One day."

TWELVE

SANTE

A few hours before.

"You're trying to push us out."

"That's not true."

"Then we should all split profits evenly," Alize argued.

"We're taking all the risk," I barked back.

"The routes you're getting puts us at a point of being in debt to you," Carmine complained.

"The routes aren't changing, and you can either vote on them or not."

"Tommaso, what do you say?" Alize pressed.

"This is bullshit. How did you pull this off?" Tommaso shouted.

"We saw a need and fulfilled it."

"He's marrying the sister of Ted Clark!" Carmine shouted, and I held a hand at Renato's chest to hold him back.

"What is he talking about, Sante?"

"Carmine doesn't know himself."

"I have it on good authority that he's trying to double cross all of us."

"We have the final numbers if you want to go there and cause problems, Carmine," Renato seethed.

"Renato, threats will not be tolerated at the table," Tommaso remarked. I chucked my chin up for him to listen and calm down.

"I want to know more about his woman."

"She's not a concern for you."

"Something's special about her," Carmine taunted, and I charged over the table, Renato held me back.

"Shut the fuck up about her!" I pushed Renato off me.

"Someone's angry. Maybe Rena would like to come over to my side. We have a connection. I can feel it."

"What?"

"Oh, she didn't tell you."

"Spit it out, Carmine."

Carmine tapped his hand on the table.

"We met up the other day. Well, more like we ran into each other."

"Met up where?"

"At the gas station. She was looking good, and her soft lips tasted better than I'd imagined." Carmine teased, and I reached in the back of the holster for my gun.

"Sante!" Alize, Tommaso, and Renato all called my name at the same time.

"Keep her name out of your mouth."

"I think he's unhinged, Alize," Carmine stated.

"Fuck you."

"Whoever this woman is, she'd got you making choices that are viable to our business." Alize implied, and I waved off his concern.

"Renato, let's go before I do something I won't regret."

"Tell Rena I'll be seeing her again." Carmine grinned.

Normally, nothing got to me from a rival boss, but he'd pushed a button I tried to keep telling myself wasn't real. We stomped out of the room and back to the car. I climbed in and told Danny to head home.

"What are you going to do?"

"Find out what the hell he's talking about."

"Try to calm down first."

"I am calm."

"Your knuckles are turning red. I'm surprised you didn't punch him."

"I really wanted to kill that asshole."

"He's bluffing."

"You think they kissed?"

"Hell no. Rena's too uptight to go around kissing strangers, let alone Carmine."

"How do you know?"

"We've talked."

"You and Rena."

"She's down to earth, once you get over her high maintenance ideas."

The smile that came to my face on its own told me I was coming undone by this woman, and I didn't like that.

I STEPPED in the house and walked down the hall to the guest room and didn't see her, but the bathroom light was on. I started to knock when I heard her over the phone.

"Do you love Sante?"

She didn't answer, which reminded me of Carmine's accusation. I shut the door to control my temper and gather my thoughts. Thoughts of a stiff drink popped in my head, and I grabbed the bottle of whiskey and a glass poured half an amount. Rena was standing in only a towel, with her hair pinned up away from her face. My eyes drank in her full frame, down to her red nail polish. She squeezed the top of the towel, shifted from the left to her right foot. I took the shot straight down, licked my lips, and placed it on the counter, then opened the bottle to pour another shout.

"I thought I heard something."

"Did you kiss Carmine?"

"Huh?"

"Did you meet up with Carmine at a gas station the other day?"

After searching her mind for a moment, her gaze finally settled on my question.

"It's not what you think."

"What do I think, Rena?" I sniffed the whiskey and took another sip. I stood from the counter and stalked nearer to her.

"He approached me."

"Taste this." Her eyes glanced at the cup, then back at me as I pressed it to her lips. Her hands fell on top of mine. Her lips spread, and her tongue eased out, as I found my dick stiffened in in my pants.

"About what?" I took the glass back and finished off the last sip

"Basically, how he's going to kill you."

"Do you believe him?"

"No."

"He said you kissed."

"That's a lie."

"Is it... I mean you've flirted with my brother and every—"

Her eyes darkened in response.

"Carmine isn't my type, and if he were, I wouldn't kiss him."

"Why not?"

"Because he's threatened to kill my family."

"You expect me to believe that."

"Believe whatever you want, and if I did kiss anyone, why do you care?"

"Because you're going to be a wife!"

"You were the one that said it's not real!" She started to storm off, but I reached out and grabbed her by the hand to pull her into my chest.

"I'm sorry," I whispered, cupped her face, and wiped the tear away from her cheek.

"Sante... I..."

I caressed her cheek.

"What, baby?"

Rena whimpered in my hold, as she planted her hands around my arm.

"Kiss me."

"Can this be real?" Then I kissed her neck, along with her lips.

"Yes."

The back-and-forth dance for the past few months built up to this moment, and I prayed she allowed me to please her.

"Can I make love to you?"

"Yes."

I grasped both ends of the towel, allowing it to fall to the floor.

"I don't want to fight what's between us anymore."

"The marriage."

"Tomorrow, I want to marry you tomorrow and show you how much I've grown to care for you, even love you."

Suddenly, our lips met, and I bent down to lift her. I wrapped her legs around my waist and kissed her once more. Afterward, we retired to my bedroom. I kicked the door open and laid her on my bed and reached in my pants to remove the condom from my wallet. Hovering over her body, my hand lingered slowly across her chest. The taste of her hardened nipple gave me goosebumps. Her scent was unbearable, and her moans had me in a trance. To think Carmine was anywhere near her caused a sharp pain in my chest. I closed my eyes to calm myself down. Her back arched off the bed, and Rena moved a slender hand up to my head and directed my movements. I responded and moved my index finger to her sex, sliding her lips open and teasing her clit.

"No going back, Rena. Are we clear?"

Her eyes flickered, and she nodded.

"I need you to tell me, cara. Do you want this for real?"

"Yes!" she whined, as I eased inside her. I pushed her legs wider with my own and continued to pump in and out with my finger, as she wet my entire hand. Her breath grew louder, and I matched her moans with my own at the feel of her sweet arousal.

"Shit, you feel good, baby."

"Please... I can't take it anymore."

"We're only on the first step."

Swiftly switching my finger for my tongue and teased her nub, I watched her squeeze her breasts, eyes drifting down on me. My tongue pushed deeper, and she cried out. This was the best liquid I'd ever had on my tongue.

"Arghhh!" she whimpered, with her eyes shut closed, and her mouth dropped agape.

"Our love won't be easy."

"I don't care," she panted, popping her eyes open.

"Baby... you're so tight."

Her limbs convulsed in my arms when I slid my tongue into her ass. At this moment, I couldn't wait to not use condoms for the first time in my life, feeling her body against my own.

"Hold onto me."

I grabbed the condom, pushed my pants down, guided the base of my dick to her wet opening, and pushed forward. Slowly I eased in one inch at a time, until her warmth held me in a tight grip. My life had never been the same since I met her. There had been no other feelings like this with any woman I had known before.

"Ohhh... fuck," she groaned, as I moved her hands over her head. My dick pulsed as I pushed my forehead against hers, grunting. When my chest fell on top of her, I buried even deeper in her mound.

"Rena... shit, you're so beautiful," I panted, thrusting faster. Our bodies clapped against each other. Sweat poured down my face, as an ache crept in my mind that my possessiveness would be even stronger after this.

"Never letting you go," I growled, as she screamed next to my ear. I let her hands go, and she shuddered from her own orgasm.

"I need you too," she begged, crashing her lips to mine, teasing my tongue. Not in the mood to move, I'd rather fall asleep within her sweet pussy. I nuzzled my face in her next and slowly moved in her warmth for another round.

THE NEXT MORNING, I groaned. Something felt lighter when my mind connected to the warm body lingered next to me. We had sex two more times last night. She even rode me and caused me to call her name. Normally, intimacy with a woman was me getting my release. With her, I wanted to make sure she was shown care, tenderness, and time to feel every touch. Being vulnerable with Rena would be a new challenge I was willing to do if she allowed me to be her husband, even though it was forced on her.

"Rena..." I caressed her back, turning sideways to kiss the back of her neck.

"Mhhmmm." she moaned, shifting to face me.

"I need you to listen to me."

Her eyes opened.

"What is it, Sante?"

"I need to marry you today."

She grinned, leaning in to kiss me on the lips.

"Okay."

"You'll marry me."

"Yes, I'll marry you today."

"No party or anything, just us."

"I can do that."

"Where would you like to go for a honeymoon?"

She giggled.

"Surprise."

"Surprise you?"

"Yep, if you know me so well, I want you to surprise me."

"How about you tell me?"

She laughed, and I reached over to pull on top of me.

"I need to get a dress."

"We can have some delivered for you to choose."

"Do you believe me about Carmine?"

"He was trying to get a rise out of me."

"Where did you see him?"

"Doesn't matter."

Rena reached under the sheet and gripped my dick.

"We have to get ready."

Her hand moved up and down on my dick, and her eyes rolled to the back of my head.

"Rena... shit."

"I want to be a designer."

"Designer?"

"I've always wanted to create my own clothes, and I started sketching again."

"Clothes?"

"Yes, so I'm using the money from the deal to start my business."

"What about writing for the newspaper?"

"Be honest, you got me fired, right?" She pressed a kiss on my jaw.

I smirked, and she shook her head, climbing off my lap, but I stopped her.

"Wait!"

"Nope, you're going to pay for that. So no sex until our trip."

"You're punishing yourself."

"I think I'll be fine."

"Is this how this marriage will be, Mrs. Calabresi?"

"Depends on you, Mr. Calabresi." She kissed me again, climbed out of bed, and ran to the bathroom. I shook my head and watched her ass jiggle, going into the bathroom.

CHAPTER

THIRTEEN

RENA

Hours later

I stood beside Sante at the justice of the peace wearing a sleek, silky, long, form-fitted white dress. Sante had on a black tuxedo with Elio and Renato, his best man. McKayla was on FaceTime, and Cora was here as her stand in since she and Savio couldn't be here right now.

"Do you Rena Clark take Sante Calabresi to be your wedded husband?" the clerk asked. Sante held onto my hands.

"I do." Sante pulled the back of my hand to his lips.

"Do you Sante Calabresi take Rena Clark to be your wedded wife?"

"I do."

"I now pronounce you husband and wife."

Adelina opened the bottle of champagne, which brought me out of my dream from earlier today of Sante and me getting married. I held my hand out to look at my wedding ring and smiled. She passed each of us a glass. McKayla was still wiping her tears, since her emotions

122

were still all over the place after the birth. Savio held his son in his arms, stood next to her, and whispered in her ear to get her to calm down. When we came to their home, she pouted for a few minutes before we had a chance to enjoy the moments of her new baby and my future as a wife.

"How does it feel, Rena, to be a part of the family?"

"Different."

"Have you talked to your mom?" Adelina sipped on her champagne and sat next to me on the couch. Sante stood next to his brother, but our eyes connected every few minutes.

"No. I'm going to see her afterwards."

"Even though we weren't there, and you guys skipped out on having it here, I'm happy for you."

"Sorry, Sante wanted to keep it private."

"He's always been secretive."

"Will you two have another wedding later?" McKayla reached for the glass of water, and Savio bent down to kiss her on the lips.

"He's so cute, McKayla."

"Looks exactly like Savio. I had done nothing but carry him."

"What about you two and kids?" Adelina asked. I shifted in my seat.

"Kids aren't in our future. Sante and I want to focus on ourselves."

"No children?"

"Adelina," his father scolded her.

"I'm finally taking the leap to get my career going."

"Are you going back to the newspaper?" McKayla wondered.

"Rena Fashions."

"What! Are you designing for real?" McKayla reached over and gave me a hug.

"Yes, it's taken some years, but I guess it was blessing that Sante got me fired."

"What are you doing about a honeymoon?"

"I told him to surprise me."

"Oooh, maybe he'll take you to New York."

"Anywhere is fine, but I want to get a career. Sitting around as a housewife is not my thing."

"Give it time and be patient. Get to know each other," McKayla explained.

"We will."

"You hung up on me last night. What happened?"

Squeezing my thighs together, I remembered his tongue and thick shaft between my legs last night.

"Sante and I had a talk last night."

"What about?"

"Let's talk in the kitchen." I stood, and Sante circled his arm around my waist.

"Where are you going?" he whispered, kissing my ear.

"To talk to McKayla privately. Don't worry, I'm not skipping out."

He tapped me on the butt and bit me gently on my shoulder.

"Hurry back."

"I will."

McKayla went into the kitchen, and I followed her and put the glass on the counter.

"Tell me about the talk."

"He asked me if I kissed Carmine."

"The one who tried to kill you?"

"Yes."

"But he's trying to kill you and your brother."

"I know, that's what I told him."

She turned to pull the fridge open and removed a tray of fruit and vegetables.

"Why would he think that?"

"Because somehow Carmine got in his head."

"Probably at the meeting."

"What meeting?"

"Savio told me they had a meeting to try to get the other bosses to sign off on his company."

"Carmine must have been there."

"Be careful, Rena."

"What do you mean?"

"If he's telling you to stay away from Carmine, it's for a reason."

"I'm not around Carmine; the man is trying to kill me."

"What about your brother?"

I ignored his question.

"Rena, seriously he's not a regular soldier."

"I know that."

"Do you? You're the wife of an underboss! They might seem sweet, but underneath, he's a killer like his brother."

"What are you saying?"

"Sante will show you a side of him that other people don't see, but that comes with loyalty and respect. Don't lose his respect."

"He's my brother."

"Ted will do anything to save his own ass," she hissed, removing a plastic fork from a drawer, and organized the cheese from the fruit.

I placed my hand on my forehead and rubbed the migraine that was coming on.

"We had sex last night!" I confessed, and her eyes widened.

"Before you got married?"

"McKayla, I've never been the traditional type."

"But isn't that like bad luck?"

"Only if you let it, but we're going to make this relationship work."

"I mean he's sabotaged enough of your dates in the past."

"Especially that time at the movie theater with Jason."

She laughed, and I grabbed a grape from the tray, popping in my mouth.

"You think he's serious or just because you had sex?"

"Honestly, I don't know. But it was his idea."

"Maybe it will rub off on the rest of the guys."

"Time will tell."

I carried the second tray back to the family room and talked about how we were planning to get a house once they get business squared away. I even had a chance to show pictures of my designs, which I hoped to have time to create more after Sante got the truck business up and running.

~

THE NEXT NIGHT

Sante held a bouquet of flowers in his hand. At the same time, he lifted the back of my palm to his lips and pressed a kiss. The door swung open, and Mom greeted me, then Sante.

"Come inside; the food is almost ready."

"Thank you for having me over, Ms. Clark." Sante handed the flowers over.

"Well, when my daughter told me she was planning to get married, I thought it would be nice to meet you formally."

I removed my wedding ring and slipped it in my purse before we got out of the car.

"We—"

I cut Sante off and cleared my throat.

"Mom, what did you cook?"

Both of them looked at me strangely.

"Pot roast with brussel sprouts."

"Sounds great."

"Sante, tell me what you do exactly. Last time we met still plays in my head." She motioned to the couch, and we sat, while she stood.

"My family has a business that I work at."

"Like investments?"

"Partially. We have real estate and a trucking company."

"Where did you and Rena meet?"

"Through McKayla," I blurted, giving her a look to stop with the third degree.

"Explain how Rena owes you money, but you married her."

My throat tightened in nervousness.

"Mom," I groaned.

"Ted told me it was all a lie. You've been dating a criminal."

Sante darted his eyes to me, and I felt my stomach drop.

"He's not a criminal," I lied. If she really knew him, the police would be outside her door right now.

"So, he didn't rough your brother up?

"What are you talking about?"

"Your brother came here with a black eye."

"That's bullshit! Ted probably owes someone money."

"Rena, what are you talking about?"

"Rena, calm down." Sante placed his hand on my thigh and squeezed.

"No, why are you believing him and not me."

"Because he's shown me pictures."

"What pictures?"

"Whatever your son has shown you is a lie," Sante argued.

"Do you know Ted owes so many people money, they're trying to kill me and you."

"Rena, that's ridiculous."

"How do you think he paid for this house?"

"Not about to argue with you. Your brother has taken care of the both of us for years."

"No, he helped me once, and I've been on my own since then."

"He's family."

"Sante is my family!" I reached in my purse to pull out my wedding ring and slid it on my finger.

"Rena!" she gasped, dropped the flowers on the floor, and grabbed my hand to study the ring.

"You're married."

"I hate that it came to this, but Ted is lying. I went to confront him about everything."

"This is too much." She waved me off and went to the kitchen.

"No the problem is you not supporting your daughter's marriage"

"He's not good for you."

"He's my husband."

"Men like him will only lead to pain and suffering."

"You can't compare my marriage to what my father did to you."

"Get out!" She pointed at the front door.

"What?"

"I want you to leave my home and don't come back until you're ready to apologize and end that marriage."

"Don't do this."

"While you're married to him, you can forget about having anything to do with me."

"Wow, I thought a mother's love is unconditional."

"Rena, you will not blame this on me."

"Blame it on your son."

"Just go."

"If you change your mind, I'm here."

"That goes both ways," she responded.

I stared at her for a few minutes before I turned and left the kitchen, meeting Sante at the door. He grabbed both sides of my face, kissed my forehead, and held the door open to let me out first. I felt my shoulders shudder as tears pooled in my eyes.

"He's turned her against me."

"She'll come around."

"I don't think so, Sante."

"Are you regretting today?"

"No, but how can I go on without having my mom in my life?"

"Maybe give her some space and then talk to her."

"She's stubborn like me."

"So that's where you get it from." He chuckled, and I giggled.

"I hate my brother."

"Family can be complicated sometimes."

"After everything I've done for him."

"Try to focus on what's good in your life."

"You're right."

"Ted will learn to listen on his own."

"What do you mean?"

"People like him will get arrogant and fuck up with the wrong person one day."

"You mean he'll get killed?"

He stopped at the red light and turned to me.

"Listen to me, Rena. I know he's your brother, but if I had to choose between you and him, my money is on you every time."

The light turned green, and as Sante drove off, I felt a coldness in his voice that if he tried one more thing, my brother could end up dead. I prayed that it wasn't at the hands of Sante, but Ted was determined to get payback.

FOURTEEN

A month later

Knock! Knock!

"Come in."

I pushed the pencil out of my mouth and spread the designs I'd been practicing on the bed.

"Breakfast in bed?"

"You refuse to work out of my office, like a normal person. I decided to bring you food in here." I stood and took the cup of tea off the tray and blew over it before I took a sip. He made it exactly how I love it with lemon and honey.

"Nothing wrong with the guest room."

"Except you fall asleep here most nights, then I have to carry you to bed."

I placed the cup on the nightstand and stood on my tiptoes, extending my arms around his neck.

"I like when you carry me to bed."

He slid his hands down to my ass.

"Bet you do. What are you working on?"

"A dress idea."

"You've been working on the same design for the last few nights."

"The idea is stuck in my head, and I need to make it perfect."

"Come eat first."

"Not hungry."

Sante picked up the piece of bacon and angled it to my lips.

"I need you to have all your strength."

"Why?"

"Because I have a surprise for you."

"What is it?"

"You have to eat first."

"Sante, I hate surprises, babe."

"You'll love this surprise."

"Thank you for breakfast, but don't you have work you need to get to?"

"That's my surprise."

"What?"

"I'm spending the day with and taking you on a date."

"A date?"

"Yeah."

"We're already married."

"I've heard women like having dates with their husbands."

"Did McKayla tell you to take me on a date?"

He sat down on the bed, lifted me off my feet, tossed me on the bed.

"Sante!"

"Baby, this is all my idea."

"Thank you, but you've been forgiven."

"Forgiven."

"For the marriage situation."

"Why are you forgiving?"

"I think deep down I've liked you for the longest and felt a little resentment that you never admitted your feelings."

"Baby."

"No, let me explain."

"Go ahead."

"This deal at first felt like a little sting to my heart."

"I cared for you, Rena."

"Does that lead to love?"

He stared at me, and I could admit my feelings ran deep, but I wouldn't force him to admit something he wasn't ready to admit.

"Love is a crazy word in my lifestyle, but I can admit my heart is yours to break, so I hope you take extra care. There is no one else for me."

Our kiss grew intense, and I had to nudge him back to let me up.

"I'm hungry."

"Crazy as usual." He tapped me on the ass, I grabbed the plate of pancakes, sausage, and fruit.

"Tell me what you planned today."

"We'll start with shopping and then dinner."

"How should I dress for dinner?"

"Nothing too revealing." I nibbled on his neck.

"Okay..." I sighed, feeling his hand move up to my sex.

"Finish eating and meet me in the front in fifteen minutes."

I watched him leave the room and cut into the pancakes.

Ring!

"Hey, Ted."

"Rena, how are you?"

"What do you want, Ted?"

"I can't call my sister?"

"Usually it means you're up to something."

Ted laughed on the other end of the phone.

"That's fair."

"How can I help you, Senator?"

"I'd love to meet and talk."

"Why?"

"Mom called me."

"Did she?"

"She's hurting."

"Because you lied."

"He's dangerous."

"Coming from you, that doesn't make me feel confident."

"He wants to kill your family."

"Sante would never hurt you. Yes, he threatened you, but things are working out now."

"Please tell me you don't believe that."

"I believe he gave you a chance to save your ass, and you threw me under the bus."

"Rena, you're being foolish."

"Ted, I'm going to hang up."

"All right. Can you meet me, and we can talk?"

"No, I'm slammed with work right now."

"The little newspaper job can wait."

"I don't work there anymore. I'm designing now."

"He's allowing you to work?"

"No one allows me to do anything. Sante supports my dreams."

"Sorry, Rena. Honestly, just meet me."

"When I get caught up on work, I'll think about contacting you. Don't call me again." I hung up and tossed the fork and knife on the plate, not feeling hungry anymore. When I rose from the bed and took the tray back into the kitchen, I saw Sante with his guards. I went to grab my jacket and slid my feet in a pair of shoes.

"You all right?" He noticed my sour mood, and I felt bad for not eating the rest of the food he cooked.

"Just an upset stomach," I lied again. We promised to be honest, especially with Ted contacting me. The honeymoon phase would leave us soon, and I didn't want him to cause more problems.

"Do you want to stay home?"

"No, shopping is my therapy."

"We can have clothes delivered."

"Really?"

"Yeah, remember you're married to billionaire, babe." He pinched my cheek.

"Actually, let's have the dresses delivered and watch movies until later. Then we can go out for dinner."

"Anything you wish."

He helped to remove my jacket, and I popped the shoes off and put them in the corner as his guards left the room.

"Call me when they get here!"

"Where are you going?"

"To finish the designs."

LATER THAT EVENING, Sante reached a hand toward me to grab the car door. I stepped out of the Mercedes Benz, and he smiled at me. Rarely did he drive, but his guards trailed us to the location. He'd also taken the extra step of buying out the restaurant for us to have it alone. The door of Catarina's Italian Restaurant opened, and we thanked the hostess who motioned for us to follow her to our table.

"Mr. and Mrs. Calabresi, we have your meal all set for you this evening."

"Thank you, Delaney."

"Would you like for me to pour your wine?" She picked up the bottle from the ice bucket.

"Please."

Delaney filled both glasses, then left us alone.

"This place is beautiful, Sante."

"I'm glad you like the place."

"Today has been great all around."

"Glad you enjoyed spending my money." I laughed, and he lifted the glass up.

"Well, being married to a billionaire comes with perks."

"Most certainly does."

"What are we toasting?'"

Our hands clasped together; my right hand held my glass of red wine.

"To you and your dreams becoming reality, for what the future holds."

Clink!

The wine soothed down my throat, and I felt myself on a high at how far he'd changed over the past few weeks. The arrogant, jealous, mafia boss shed the past behind him and showed me that love was something I could strive for, long as it was with the right person.

"The hostess said you have a pre-menu picked."

"All things you'll love from fettuccine, veal, and gnocchi dishes."

"I'm starving."

"There's something I wanted to talk to you about."

"Tell me."

Delaney came to our table with our dishes.

"First serving is fettuccine, caviar, and a side of bread." Delaney laid the plates down, and I planted the napkin on my lap.

"Thank you, Delaney."

"You were saying, husband?" I teased, picking over my food.

"I want to stop using condoms."

The words he spoke made me freeze in place. He'd had the same thoughts as I, and I was afraid to bring them up.

"I've always used condoms, but with you, I want to be free and feel you fully."

"Okay."

"So, it will stop tonight."

"I was thinking the same thing as you, but I was too afraid to bring it up."

"You've never been shy with me, Rena."

"The thought came up, but I figured you'd shut it down because most men in your position think someone is after your money."

"Hey, you never have to think about me in that way. Our relationship even before all this, I knew you could be trusted."

"Even when I kept pushing your buttons."

"Those days when you were staying with me and walked around in only shorts and a sports bra were hard."

He winked a left eye at me.

"I have to tell you something."

The smile he wore dropped from his face.

"Ted called me today."

His jaw ticked.

"About what?"

"He told me that I should leave you."

"Ted's a big boy. When did he care about you?"

"I think it has to do with my mom."

"Y'all haven't talked since at dinner that night."

"I told him you aren't threatening him anymore, and we've become a real couple."

"Ted will always be for Ted. You can't trust him, Rena."

"Funny, he said the same thing about you."

"Do you believe him? I mean, are we just fooling ourselves?"

"No."

"Then why are you taking his calls? Ted will do and say anything to make me look bad."

"He's my only family."

"Family who would have you killed if it could save his life."

There was a tense look between us, then I dropped my fork and rubbed the top of his palm.

"Tonight should be about us. I'm sorry for bringing him up."

"I have another surprise for you."

"Sante, you're spoiling me."

"You deserve to be spoiled.

None of this was a fairytale, but Sante was close to being my Prince Charming. I just wished it came from a different situation.

"When we get home, I want you to pack."

"Where are we going?"

"It's a surprise."

"How do I know what to pack?"

"Something warm, but a few items that you can wear without a coat."

"How long will we be gone?"

"A few days. I have business to handle when I get back."

"Like a week or less."

"A week."

I sat up a little, cuffed his chin, and slid my tongue in his mouth to thank him for tonight and the upcoming trip he'd planned all by himself for just the two of us alone.

"No longer hungry for food."

"What do you have in mind, Rena?"

"Your dick in my mouth," I teased, sipping on the glass of wine, and peered at him.

CHAPTER

FIFTEEN

RENA

Two days later in Paris

The staff and management did everything to make us comfortable here in Paris. Sante rented the top floor of the Four Seasons George V. Paris. Everything was elegant and luxurious, reminding me of classic Paris old school Grace Kelly. Our bags were left next to the door, as I looked out the window as cars rode by.

"What do you think?"

I swung around to Sante.

"Happy to be here and experience this with you."

"Glad you came with no issue."

"Am I that hard to convince?"

"Sometimes, unless I have you at my mercy, calling my name."

"Mhmmm... I like the sound of that."

"We'll get to that, but first, I want to show you around Paris."

"Show me."

"A visit with some very important people."

"Like whom?"

"The fashion houses."

"Wait... Fashion houses." I jerked back from him.

"You get a walk through with fashion designer Abigail Felnozi."

"You're kidding."

"No, I set up for you to go to the fashion show."

"How is that possible?"

"Your husband made it possible."

"But..."

"No questions. I want you to enjoy this and then go sightseeing."

"Let me grab my purse." Excitedly, I released him, running to grab my purse and phone for pictures.

"Do you know how much I love her designs?"

"Didn't know, but I wanted to give you a chance to see what all goes on with a fashion show."

"Thank you, Sante."

"No need to thank me."

"All of this wouldn't be possible without you."

"Later you can thank me."

"Will you let me be in control?'' He was known to be in control no matter the situation, but if I had one chance to make him lose control, that would be the best moment I could ever have in our marriage.

"Depends."

"On what?"

"How many times can I make you come?"

Sante turned me down and had me wet already, but I had to be at the fashion spot before the day got away from me.

"Save that for later."

"I thought you'd see it my way." He laughed, and I

slapped him on the shoulder. Sante locked the door behind us and strolled down the hall to the elevator, with our mouths connected, ignoring everyone around us.

"Hmmmm…" he moaned into my mouth, backing me up against the corner of the elevator as we entered.

Ding!

Five minutes later, we walked out of the elevator a little disheveled after Sante had me up against the wall with my panties slid to the side, and his finger plunging into my wetness. Our driver was waiting for us.

"I need to call McKayla."

"Have you talked to her since we arrived?"

"No, and I feel bad."

"Take pictures. I'm sure she'll understand."

"Yeah, having a newborn keeps her pretty busy."

"Savio said he's sleeping through the night."

"Are you regretting us not having kids?" I chewed on my bottom lip.

"Where is that coming from?"

"I wonder if you have regrets."

"Only regret is not making us a couple sooner."

He brushed a hand on top of mine.

"The first stop, Danny, is the Abigail Felnozi office."

Realizing Danny, his usual driver, was with us surprised me.

"You flew Danny out here?"

"Danny and a few guards are here."

"You're paranoid, babe?"

"Have to make sure the most important person with me is protected."

We kissed briefly, then stared at the beautiful scenery as the car drove through the streets of Paris. Forty minutes later, we arrived at the studio of Felnozi. I opened the door and waited for Sante to get out, but he lingered back.

"Are you coming with me?"

"No, this is your thing. I have a few things to set up for us. You have fun."

"I'm going to miss you."

"Try not to get in too much trouble."

"You're leaving me without protection."

"Always have protection, *cara*." Sante tapped on the door, and the car drove off.

The door opened, and Abigail herself stood there with the most stylish gown I'd ever seen.

"Abigail Felnozi?"

"Mrs. Calabresi, nice to meet you."

"You too. Thank you for the chance to be here."

"Come inside. Sante speaks highly of you."

"You know my husband?"

"Not that familiar, but he's very convincing."

I chuckled at her comment. He more than likely paid a hefty penny for this visit.

"Does all of your work get made here?"

"It does."

Abigail's studio was two stories high, all black with no sign out front besides the address. Inside, she had a regular office setting with a reception desk and offices on both ends. Abigail escorted me through the hall, arriving in front of the employee area only. The entire section housed designs and walls of pictures from previous fashion shows.

"Wow, these are gorgeous."

"Your husband told me you're preparing your own line."

"Well, I hope I have enough talent to compare to you

one day."

"Never compare yourself to me. We're all talented on our own."

"These pieces really stand out."

Each dress was cut and styled for everyday women. It didn't matter the size in a variety of colors and shapes.

"This line will be scrapped more than likely." Abigail held her glasses up against her lip.

"I wouldn't scrap everything. Maybe put it together where it's a color coordinated or by style."

"Sounds like I should hire you," she joked.

"I love clothes, mixing and matching."

"Then you'll do fine. You have the confidence."

"Thank you, Abigail."

"Come check out this one." Abigail walked over to a color pallet of flowers, with celebrities matched against the board.

"The Met Gala was last year, and I had three stars I designed."

"I remember this. You had everyone set for perfection."

"Takes a village, but we made it work."

"One day hopefully, I'll be saying the same thing."

"You will."

She laid her hand on my elbow, and we continued to discuss my goals and the process of creating a clothing label.

~

"Rena!" he pleaded, backing up further against the shower wall and tightening his hand around my wet hair, and shoved himself down my throat further. My eyes fluttered. He was surprised when I came back to the hotel and surprised him with a thank you for the day I had with Abigail. I ran a hand up his thighs with my nails, pulled his shaft out, kissed the tip, tapped it against my tongue, and licked across his balls that needed release.

"How nasty do you want it, husband?"

His head bent down to stare at me, as the water poured down my back.

"I want my wife as nasty as possible."

"Anything to please you." I trailed kisses around his balls, sucked them into my mouth, popped them out, and licked across his scrotum.

"Fuck!" He released before I could catch his seeds.

Sante's chest rose and fell, as he gripped my shoulders and pulled me to his chest, smacking me on the ass and sucking on my neck. He then gripped my breasts and turned me around to slide into my mound. He fucked me for the rest of the night.

CHAPTER

SIXTEEN

SANTE

Two days later

Soon after Rena made me come, we'd been stuck in the hotel, having sex nonstop. Our activities were cut short because all we did was eat and sleep right after. Today was the final day in Paris, and I gave her free rein on shopping with no limit. Danny walked alongside us, carrying her bags. This Gucci store was the last stop so she could pick a few things for SJ and McKayla.

"What do you think of these shoes, Sante?" Rena held baby shoes up that would probably not even fit SJ's feet since he was still too young.

"Anything for SJ."

She held onto them and moved over to the belt area. I stayed quiet to let her have fun splurging. To experience her in this state was amazing. Most women would be ready to buy a car or houses with my money. Rena only thought of buying for other people, and it made me love her more.

"Babe, come here." She held up a man's belt.

"You should be buying stuff for yourself."

"I have enough."

"Basically, you're spending my money to buy me a gift," I joked, and she stuck her tongue out at me.

"Act surprised when it shows up in your drawer."

"Anything you say *cara*."

"Can we go to the Eiffel Tower next?"

"Eiffel Tower, then we have to catch our flight."

"Do we really have to go back home?"

"We have the charity ball."

"Charity ball?"

"The event that all families have to attend. The bosses and underbosses bring their wives."

"Is it mandatory?"

Rena picked over the purses and found what she liked.

"At the position Savio and I are at, we have to show our faces."

"I guess I will be at the ball."

RENA ASKED Danny to take a picture of us in front of the Eiffel Tower after we came down from visiting the top and looked over the city. I held her in my arms and smiled again when she posed right in front of me.

"Are you hungry?"

"We can head back to the hotel and pack up."

"The plane is gassed up."

"This has been a wonderful trip, Sante. I appreciate you."

"You don't have to keep thanking me." I rubbed her chin.

"I'll probably sleep on the plane."

"All right, let's get to the hotel, order room service, and pack."

"Okay. I have so many pictures to organize. We can make this our annual visit."

"Next, we can explore an island."

"Ohh, that would be sexy. Maybe the two of us naked on the beach." Rena fondled my dick.

"Keep touching me like this, and I'll fuck you in public."

We locked eyes, and she bit her bottom lip.

"We can make some memories."

I cupped both sides of her face and lathered kisses across her cheek. Twenty minutes later, I pushed the door of the hotel room open and dropped some of our bags near the door. Rena took her bags over to the table.

"What do you have a taste for dinner?" Rena pressed.

"Whatever you get is fine." I removed my jacket, grabbed the phone out of my pocket, and checked any messages. Then I dialed my pilots to make sure everything was lined up for us to fly out tonight.

"Mr. Calabresi, we're waiting for you."

"Tom, are fresh flowers and drinks prepared?"

"Yes, sir. We filled the plane up with all of your requests."

"Danny has most of our bags packed up, so we should arrive in two hours."

"We'll be ready, sir."

"Thanks, Tom."

Ending the call, I dropped my phone on the table, watching Rena talk animatedly on the phone to I assumed was McKayla.

"We have so many clothes for SJ. I can't wait to see him dressed up."

"I wish I could have come," McKayla whined through the phone.

"Maybe the boys will let us do a girls trip one day," Rena mentioned, winking her left eye at me. I shook my head, causing her to poke out her lip.

"Have you met our husbands? Savio hates for me to even go to the grocery store by myself." McKayla blew out a breath.

"Yeah, men are protective."

"Very."

"Rena, did you order dinner?" I called out.

"McKayla let me get off the phone before he puts me on punishment," Rena teased.

"Hi, Sante!" McKayla shouted, and I chuckled.

Rena hung up and picked up the menu. As I stood at the window, darkness overtook the city. The lights were beautiful.

"What are you thinking about?" Rena came up behind me and circled her arms around my waist.

"How lucky I get to wake up to you every day."

"I feel the same way."

"Life is just beginning, Rena."

"I agree."

"So, believe me when I say, don't let anything come between us."

"I won't."

"Marriages stand the test of time because couples keep people out of their marriage."

"I agree."

I shifted her to face me.

"That means family as well."

"What's wrong?"

"Nothing. I just need you to be on my team."

"I am, Sante. Anything you need, I promise to give you my support."

"Your brother."

She paused at my words.

"He knows I'm committed to you."

"My wife is beautiful."

"Thank you." We kissed for a few seconds, until we were interrupted by the door ringing.

"That must be room service."

"I got it." Rena moved toward the door, motioning for the room service to bring the table closer.

I strolled to the table, picked up the lid, and smelled the aromas of French food. Once she paid, we sat and talked more about her ideas for designs and when we could come back to visit.

SEVERAL HOURS LATER, we made it back home to Chicago, and I traced my thumb over her cheekbones and brows as we sat in the limo coming back from the airport. Her light snores tempted me to not disturb her, but after our time together in Paris, I needed to be inside her again, to feel her soft lips against my firm, hardened member.

"Rena," I whispered to not frighten her.

"Mmmmm," she moaned and started to come out of her slumber.

"We're home."

"Did I sleep the entire flight?"

"Yeah, but you needed to rest."

The limo door opened. I climbed out and held a hand

for Rena. We sauntered in the building, while the guards brought in our bags. Stepping on the elevator while still holding hands, we pushed the button for our floor.

"I hope you're rested."

"Depends."

"On what?" Her eyes perked up.

"When we get in this house, I'll show you."

Ding!

Feverishly, I lifted her up in my arms, which caused her to gasp in surprise and look at me in awe.

"My turn to please you," I growled, brushing the tip of my tongue across her top lip. Her lips parted from my intrusion. Rena ran a finger through my hair in desperation, driving me wild. My hands ran upwards under the hem of her shirt to her warm skin. She sucked in a sharky breath. I moved my mouth slowly, biting her left breast through her shirt.

"Ughhh, Sante."

We then stumbled to the bedroom, and I held her up against the wall. Her skin tingled at my touch as I helped her stand at full height to remove her shirt and pants and kicked off the shoes. Taking my cue, she helped me to unbuckle my pants, removed my shirt, and pressed her hand against my swollen shaft. My breath rushed out of me as the intense pleasure clawed up my spine. The urge to bury myself in her slick heat soared in my mind. Rena leapt into my arms and arched her back. My tongue flicked across her nipple, teasing.

We moved over to the bed, peppering kisses to her inner thighs. She buckled against my hands that palmed her sensitive warm core. Blood surged through me, as I took hold and rubbed over her smooth skin, down to her inner thigh.

"I love you, Sante, so much," she whimpered and slid from her lips.

Desire sizzled in my chest at her words.

"What did you say?"

"I love you."

"I love you, mi amore."

With both hands closed around her waist, I slid through her walls. Her breath ragged and shallow, she clawed at my arms. Dipping my head down, I hovered my lips over hers, she cried out my name and weighed against me.

"All I can think about, Rena, is your soft lips and sexy voice."

"Yes! Fuck me, Sante," she hissed at my deep stroke. I was drunk. Sweat beads covered her breasts and the bed. Sounds covered throughout the room of two people hungry for each other, not ready to let go. Her palm drifted to my thigh, her teeth nipping at my shoulder. It was intoxicating to have a love so powerful, you'd kill anyone to not let it interfere. Thrusting upwards frantically, my head pounded with lust.

"Oh... God... keep going!" she shouted. Abruptly pulling out of her, I rotated her around to get on her knees. I reached in the drawer and grabbed the lube, poured a small amount on my dick and her tight hole. During our time in Paris, we explored anal with her wanting to try new things. I told her it wasn't something she had to do to please me, but she wanted to try it for herself. I kissed both cheeks gently and ran my tongue in and out to soothe the pressure.

"Mhmmmm..."

"All day, this ass has teased me."

"Then make me beg."

"Remember you said those words." Spreading her legs a little further, she arched her back, as I lined up with her entrance and pushed through the ring barrier. She tensed up and soothingly, I caressed both cheeks, rocking back and forth.

"You're going to come for me."

"Ahhhh!"

I picked up the pace and felt her juices drip down her thighs, covering my balls. A roar left my mouth, and I was drained as we both came.

"Arghhhh! Fuck."

A strange stab came in a flash. I worried if this was the last time we'd be happy like this or if darkness was looming to destroy what we built. I slid out of her and fell on the bed. I wrapped an arm around her waist and laid her on my chest, kissing her forehead, nose, cheek, and lips.

"That was intense."

"You bring that out of me."

"Oftentimes, you say I drive you crazy."

"That's true."

"It was like an electric current whenever we have sex."

She brushed a hand through her hair.

"When do you have to go to the office?" She ran a hand up to my shoulder.

"Before the charity ball tomorrow."

"I might go visit McKayla and the baby if you'll be up working."

"Right now, I just want to stay like this with you."

"You're becoming spoiled like SJ."

I grinned.

"Oh, I'm better at sleeping through the night when I get these." I lifted her breasts.

A flush of ecstasy appeared on her face.

"Maybe SJ can wait until tomorrow for his gifts."

"I like the way you think, beautiful."

"My turn to put you to sleep."

My heartbeat accelerated when she moved down my stomach, wrapping both hands around my dick, and spat on the tip and sucked it in her mouth. Dark eyes studied her with an intensity that would make her skin melt. This woman would one day know the real darkness that laid beneath me.

CHAPTER

SEVENTEEN

RENA

SJ's features started to take hold, and he was a combination of McKayla and Savio, with the personality of his dad. I wondered if Savio would make his child get into the business like their father did or give him the choice to figure out life on his own. McKayla didn't seem too worried when she found out she was pregnant, which was surprising considering the way she ran away after the kidnapping.

"He's going to cling to you more and more." A thin smile touched her lips.

"He knows it's his godmother."

"Adelina keeps him on her chest no matter what she's doing when she tries to babysit."

"Really?"

McKayla folded the baby clothes and nodded. The house was quiet today with all the men out at the office to prepare for the ball.

"Have you decided what you're wearing?"

"Between two dresses that I pray I can fit into," McKayla spoke through her pursed lips.

155

"Give yourself a break, McKayla. You have a baby."

"I know that in my heart, but my mind is like, 'Does Savio still want me?'" Her voice cracked.

"You're kidding, right?"

"That man wouldn't even let you hang out with me. The first time you two got together, do you know how possessive he was over you?"

"Because he needed me for something."

"Yeah, you're his heart, breath, and lungs. He would kill anything that interrupts your happiness."

"Sounds like him." She chuckled.

"Don't stress yourself out. Savio loves you more than himself, but I finally made up my mind while I was in Paris."

McKayla sat on the bed, piling SJ's clothes together.

"I'm going to get back into designing and launch my fashion brand."

"You have talent, Rena. I never understood why you got so upset with Samira."

"She didn't have to fire me like that." I snuggled my nose in SJ's neck.

"Well, everyone got what they wanted in the end."

"How about we go out to eat? The three of us."

"I need to check with Savio."

"McKayla, it's lunch. What harm can it do? Plus, we can invite Adelina."

"You're right. I need to get out more." McKayla jumped up, grabbed the clothes, and placed them in the closet, then whipped around to take SJ out of my hold to change his clothes. I reached in my pocket for my phone and dialed Nikki to see if she was still in New York.

"Mrs. Calabresi."

I giggled at her introduction.

"Fine, Nikki, what city are you in now?"

"Houston, to pick up a few pieces."

"Sounds like fun."

SJ started crying, so McKayla picked him up and lifted her shirt to breastfeed him.

"I was calling for a reason."

"All ears."

"I just got back from Paris. Sante surprised me with a trip to meet Abigail Felnozi."

"You're kidding!" She took in a sharp breath.

"Nope. We talked about a few things, and one was my clothing line."

"So, you're doing it for real?"

"Yes, and I hope you'll work with me on getting it started."

"You know I will."

"Thanks, Nikki. This means a lot to me."

"I can't wait to see your name on billboards."

"Well, see my name on billboards for the right reasons." I grunted, reminded of Ted's bullshit.

"Yeah, I saw pictures of you and Sante, talking about your connection to Ted."

"My life has exploded overnight."

"The ripple effect of love."

"The cause and the cure," I muttered.

"Once I get back to New York, we can talk more and then make plans for me to fly out to Chicago," Nikki informed me.

"Great. In the meantime, I will email some ideas to your inbox."

"I'm proud of you, Rena."

"Thanks again, Nikki."

"What did she say?"

"She's onboard."

"That's wonderful. This is a cause for celebration." McKayla removed SJ from her breast, patted his back, and cleaned him up, before passing him to me while she got cleaned up.

Catarina's was busy, but they made accommodations for us to sit at the back table near the corner area, closest to the privacy section. Adelina pushed SJ's stroller, and McKayla carried his bag, then set it down near the edge of the table. Our four guards had a table in front to watch the surrounding sections, yet at the same time giving us privacy. Adelina was ecstatic when I called her to come out for lunch with us. She'd been planning for the charity ball since we cancelled the official wedding at the house and got married at the courthouse.

"Adelina, what are you wearing for the charity ball?" McKayla asked.

Delaney was our server again. She approached the table with menus.

"Hi, everyone. I'm Delaney, and I'll be your server today."

"Delaney, can I have a sparkling water please." Adelina requested and opened the menu.

"Yes, Mrs. Calabresi. Anything for you two?" Delaney probed.

"Can I get a white Russian?" I quipped.

"Pretty early for alcohol, Rena." McKayla poked at me.

"You're jealous you can't," I teased and stuck out my tongue.

McKayla waved me off, and I laughed.

"These two are a mess." Adelina chortled, and Delaney laughed.

"I'll take a sparkling water as well," McKayla responded.

"Coming right up." Delaney swung around to get our drinks from the bar.

"So, the colors for the ball are red and black. I hope you two have your dresses picked out," Adelina said, glancing from me to McKayla.

Delaney appeared with our drinks, and we ordered our food.

"I have a black dress with long sleeves, with a train and an open back."

"What about you, McKayla?"

"Maybe one of those high-waisted, strapless, black cocktail dresses," McKayla answered.

"That'll be cute on you," I praised her.

"How was Paris?" Adelina asked. Delaney arrived with our food of veal, calamari, and pasta.

"Here we go, ladies." Delaney placed a plate down in front of me, then Adelina.

"Thank you," McKayla responded, grabbed her napkin, and peeked at SJ sleeping in the stroller.

"Sante had everything arranged from restaurants, museums, and shopping."

"He said you two enjoyed yourself." Adelina cut into her pasta.

"He made it worthwhile."

"I bet."

"So should we be expecting kids anytime soon?" Adelina pressed, and I choked on my water.

"Uhmmm... kids."

"You're still young; you have plenty of time to have a

career and children," Adelina remarked, and I didn't know how to tell her I wasn't interested in children. Sante and I were content with it being just the two of us.

"Well…"

"McKayla, we need to go." A guard ran up to the table.

"Why? Is something wrong with Savio?" McKayla stood from the table, reaching to pick up SJ, and he stopped her.

"I'll grab him. Press is out front. It was leaked that you're all here."

"Shit," I cursed, dropped my napkin on the table, and grabbed my purse.

"Cover SJ up," Adelina demanded. McKayla picked up the baby bag and removed the blanket to cover him up.

"Stay behind me," Anthony demanded.

He was the head bodyguard for McKayla that Savio arranged. With a military background, Anthony commanded his men to be on both sides of us, one behind. When he pushed the door open, a barrage of photographers and reporters clamored to get a photo or ask a question.

"Is it true, Rena, that your husband threatened your family?" a reporter probed, shoving the microphone in my face.

"Get out of my face!" I smacked the camera away.

"Come on! We know you used to work at the Gazette reporting the news. Now you're a mob wife," another photographer shouted.

The car door flew wide open, and Anthony helped McKayla and Adelina inside, before walking around to the passenger side of the limo.

"No comment."

I climbed in beside Adelina, as more flashes went off.

"*Does your brother have a gambling problem!*" the same photographer shouted through the closed door. The limo drove off into traffic with so many thoughts running in my head. Today was supposed to be fun and joyful.

"Ignore them, Rena."

I sniffed, sitting up in the seat.

"Is this what you go through with Savio?"

"Honestly, it never ends."

"She's right," Adelina remarked.

"Adelina, you too?"

Adelina raised her head up.

"Living in Italy, we didn't have as much intrusion from the press, but when we came here, it was like night and day," Adelina expressed.

"How was Sante growing up?"

"Intelligent, fierce, strong like his father, and protective," Adelina recalled, looking out the window.

"He's going to be pissed about today."

"The ball is tomorrow, let it go and relax," Adelina responded and patted my leg.

"Hopefully that's not eventful."

CHAPTER

EIGHTEEN

SANTE

Our guards carefully surveyed the area, while more couples arrived for the annual charity event that Savio threw to help benefit local charities. Police on our payroll were here undercover, plus our own guards lined the walls of the ballroom. Calabresi gave back to many hospitals and homeless shelters in the city and around the world.

"He's here," Renato stated, tilting his head to the right at the front door. All head bosses were permitted to attend. It was all about standing within each family, and if someone didn't show, it would be a statement of disrespect, acknowledging that you'd be stripped of your votes.

"Who did he bring?" My head swiveled around my family to Carmine standing at the front entrance with a woman I'd never seen before.

"Some blond bimbo," Renato growled, jaw ticked.

"Guards?"

"I counted four, but we never know."

"For now, we watch. He can't be stupid enough to do something right now."

"Boys, what's distracting you from the fun?" Father remarked, holding two glasses of whiskey.

"Carmine is here."

"He's the Don of Colombo family. We can't let that get under our skin."

"I'm ready to kill him," Renato hissed, swallowing his drink.

"Not tonight, Renato," Father demanded.

"Where's Savio?" Renato asked, scanned the room.

"He's talking to the mayor."

I focused on Carmine shaking hands nearby, and strolled through the crowd up to us.

"Sante, we still need to talk." Alize appeared next to us.

"Alize, no business tonight." Father pushed a glass in his hand.

"You know I respect the Calabresi Family, but this has gotten out of hand," Alize fussed. Carmine clapped him on the back, interrupting us.

"Well, what do we have here? Another business meeting, and Sante is trying to take over," Carmine taunted. The waiter walked by, so I dropped my glass on his tray.

"You're only invited to appear. Doesn't mean you need to speak." I stepped in front of his face.

"Now, now, big guy. I think you need to worry about that sweet little thing over there." Carmine pointed at Rena.

"Keep my wife out of your mouth."

"Carmine, you shouldn't try to cause a problem at a charity event," Father pressed.

"Maybe we should go outside and continue this conversation," Renato stated. I pressed my hand on his chest.

"With pleasure," Carmine taunted. Renato pushed him in the chest. I got between them, and a few people turned to look at us.

"Sante! What's going on?" Rena walked up and grabbed my hand. I pulled her behind me.

"Rena, Rena, sexy little Rena." Carmine tried to go around me.

"If you want to walk outside this building with both legs, you better get the fuck out of my wife's face."

"Sante..."

"Rena, hush," I barked.

"Oh, so he yells at you, Rena. Remember what I told you. I always have room for you." Carmine stopped the waiter and picked up a glass of champagne.

"Motherfucker!" I shoved him in the chest. Rena screamed and ran off.

"Watch yourself, Sante! I won't look away if you touch me again." Carmine drank the champagne down.

"You came near my wife again and found out what happened."

"If you find she wants to be in my arms, I can assure you. I won't push her away," Carmine hinted. I raised my fist and punched him in the face. His men ran over and tried to lunge at me, but Renato gripped one guy around the next and shoved him into the wall.

"Sante!" Madre shrieked in horror.

"Where's Savio?" Father demanded, trying to comfort my mother.

All I heard were cries and screams for us to stop, but I

blacked out and went into kicking Carmine's ass. He threw a punch back, but when it knocked me down, it only motivated me more. I charged at him, and we fell over the table.

"Renato, take him out of here," Savio commanded and grabbed me around the shoulder, nudging me back.

"Where's Rena?"

"McKayla's with her," Savio quipped.

Renato passed a phone into my hand. I looked down, and he cocked his head to follow him to the corner.

"Who's phone is this?"

"Carmine."

"That bastard is ready to die."

"Look at the text thread."

I went to the messaged section and saw Ted's name upfront. My eyebrows lifted in surprise.

"*I can give you Rena as payment,*" I read off Ted's comment.

"He's trying to pawn his sister off to get rid of his debt." Renato paced back and forth.

"*I called her to meet with me, and she agreed,*" read another response from Ted.

"I need to find her."

"First, you need to calm down and not go off the rails."

"I yelled at her." I rubbed both hands down my face.

"Carmine probably planned the whole situation."

"Why would he do that?"

"To throw us off. Even these messages could be fake."

"I need permission from Savio to kill him."

"All of the bosses will have to agree, Sante."

"If they don't?"

"We're brothers. I have your back no matter what." Renato extended a hand for me to take.

"Carmine's gone." Savio walked up on us.

"Where's the girls?"

"Drinking at the table. You need to control your temper."

"I think Carmine's planning something."

"He saw what happened to Maurizio," Savio replied.

"That makes him an even bigger threat." I waved my arm out to the ballroom.

"Listen to me, don't do anything foolish. We have too much at stake."

"If this was McKayla?"

"McKayla has no bearing on this situation." Savio's eyes darkened.

"For now, I'll play by your rules, but if he does anything…"

"He has an entire message thread with Ted."

"We can't handle killing another boss of a family right now!" Savio shouted.

"That's bullshit!" I spat.

"Ted is a senator, and Carmine is a boss. The moment they go missing, cops will be in our shit!"

"We can't sit on this forever."

"I let you handle the truck deal, backed you up on every decision. Listen to me now, little brother."

I ignored his words.

"This family will not get involved, not until he makes the first move," Savio announced. I had to live with those words for the time being, but it was a greenlight that I could handle both men if something came up.

"Fine, I want someone on Ted ASAP."

"Already handled." Savio clapped me on the back and

escorted us back to our table. I sat next to Rena and kissed the side of her face. She smiled.

"Sorry about earlier," I said.

"I know."

"You'll have extra protection moving forward."

"Why?"

"Because Carmine is getting dangerous."

"Sante, that's not necessary."

"Rena, don't argue with me. This is for your protection."

"I think you're overreacting."

"Is there anything I should know about?" I searched her face.

"No, why do you ask?"

"No reason." I leaned back and circled my arm on her chair as she talked to McKayla.

~

A MONTH later

ACE Trucking today, and the media was already lined up out front. Reporters wanted a walk through, and I still needed to get last-minute details with our crew. Mostly hired up, we still needed staff for overnight, and Elio was handling that process. Vincenzo sent out invites to our board members if they wanted to attend. A few accepted, along with the mayor giving us the key to the city.

"Gentlemen, are you ready?" I stood on the loading dock in the back. We had five trucks with our logo, carrying food in some trucks, service parts in another. The real crates without guns would go in later tonight after we closed.

"Ready, boss!" one of the young drivers shouted from the back.

"Great. The mayor is going to do a little speech, then we cut the ribbon."

"It's time." The receptionist Renato hired pointed to the crowd forming out front. Bianca was five eight, with long, blond hair, large breasts, and wide hips. I informed Elio he should have been here when the decision was made, but I couldn't fire her until it became a problem.

"All right, gently line up next to your trucks. They'll get pictures, but no questions," I explained, heading to the front near the mayor.

"Mr. Calabresi, I was just saying it's a pleasure to have your family keeping jobs in this state," Mayor Lonnie Parks stated.

"Thank you, Mr. Mayor. We love to give back."

"Mr. Mayor, are you in bed with the Calabresi Family!" a reporter yelled, and I chuckled at his question.

"Omar, we're here to support local business. Nothing about this is illegal," the mayor answered.

"What about the donation to your campaign?" another one threw out.

"We're here to do an opening ceremony, guys. So, let's give it up for ACE Trucking and Sante Calabresi!" The mayor and I held onto the large scissors and cut the ribbon, while people clapped. We stood for pictures. Five minutes later, the mayor and I walked the reporters through the company and showed how we operate from the loading dock to the employee area, including the items we imported and exported through our division.

"Thank you all for coming." I waved goodbye, and the mayor stood at the window to watch them leave.

"I hope we don't have any problems from you, Sante," Lonnie said.

"Of course not, Mr. Mayor."

"I supported this business, but I don't like it one bit."

"Well, Mr. Mayor, you shouldn't have betrayed your constituents."

"Blackmail is the only way you people know how to work."

"Our money didn't seem like a problem for you either, now did it, sir?"

"If something goes wrong, I won't bail you out."

"Is that a threat?" I stalked over to get in his face."

"You have enough problems I hear."

"What the fuck does that mean?"

"Nothing at all, Sante. Again, congrats on your new adventure." Lonnie left the office, and I slammed the door shut, sighed and slid my hands in my pocket. Five minutes later, the door opened, and Renato rushed inside.

"You need to see this." He handed over his phone.

I clicked on the video and saw Carmine and Ted together.

"Where did you get this?"

"Some of Carmine's men aren't completely loyal."

"We strike now, he won't know what hit him." Carmine pointed a finger in Ted's face.

"Will that clear my debt?" Ted begged.

"I want to take everything away from that family. If you want to live, you'll help me," Carmine snapped.

I closed out the video and tapped my finger on the desk in thought.

"Where's Rena?

"At home, working."

"Good. I want men around the house at all times."

"She's going to know something is wrong if you keep her locked up."

"I'll worry about that later."

"Savio needs to know this."

"I agree. I will present it to him and my father."

"The car is waiting outside." I locked up my office, gave Bianca instructions, and followed Renato to our awaiting car.

"Did you do a background check on Bianca?"

"Yeah, why?"

"Just making sure."

"I didn't fuck her."

"Good."

"Not yet anyway."

I paused at his words and shook my head. We hopped in and sped out for the rest of the day, heading to our family home.

"Who are you calling?"

"Rena."

"Hello."

"Are you working?" I checked the time on my watch.

"Yes, Sante."

"You sound like you're annoyed with me."

"Well, you've been acting strange lately."

"Strange how?"

"Like I'm a doll that can't break."

"You're my baby doll."

"Mmmm... I like the sound of that."

"Listen, we'll have dinner tonight after I get home and watch movies."

"Are you coming home early tonight?"

"Yeah, did you have plans?"

"No, of course not. Just work."

"Then I'll see you tonight."

"See tonight. I love you."

"Love you more."

Ten minutes later, we pulled into the gate. As soon as we parked, I jumped out of the car and ran in the house without waiting for the butler.

"Savio!"

"Elio!" Renato called.

"Boys, what's the problem?" Marilyn asked as I gave her a hug.

"Looking for everyone."

"They're outside in the backyard." Marilyn pointed. We thanked her and rushed out back. McKayla sat near the pool with SJ, Savio sat next to our father, and Elio was smoking a cigar and talking.

"What's wrong?" Father lifted his head and put down his cigar.

"Can we speak in the house?" I didn't wait for them to answer, as I swung around and went to his office. All three men appeared next to Renato.

"Here is our key."

"To what, Sante?"

"Kill Carmine."

"He's on video threatening Sante, basically the whole family."

Father and Savio glanced at each other.

"You didn't want me to rush to judgment, but now we need to stop him."

"You know what this means?" Savio insisted.

"I know. It will be looked at more closely."

"The way our business works is by having allies, even the ones we hate."

"He's right, Savio. I'm about peace, but Sante is right this time. Carmine is escalating."

"Make sure it comes across like an accident."

"Ted?" Renato brought up the biggest subject.

"The IRS could take him out."

"Let them hang themselves, and we'll be the ones to give them the rope," Father announced, walking out of the office.

CHAPTER

NINETEEN

RENA

I lit the candles on the table and poured two glasses of white wine. Turning the music on low to light old jazz, I tossed the trash away and waited for Sante to arrive home. It was going on seven, and he was coming from his parents' home. Since we'd been back, I'd worked nonstop on my designs, and he'd been setting up the trucking company. My eyes gazed up as he shut the door behind him, and I smirked as he removed his jacket, marched toward me, and wrapped an arm around my waist.

"How was your day?"

"I missed you." He nipped at my collarbone.

"I see. Can we eat first?"

Slap!

I raised to my feet after he slapped me on the ass and slipped my tongue in his mouth, moaning at the sensation of his hands kneading my ass.

"Eat first."

"Did you get your work done?"

He placed me on my feet and pulled my chair out.

"I set up my domain and figured out some ideas for a website."

"This looks good."

"I love cheesesteaks, and I wanted you to try something different."

"You think I'm stuck up?"

"Babe, you wear a lot of suits," I joked, and he hovered over the table, gripped my chin, and kissed my forehead.

"I need to talk to you about something."

I passed the ketchup to his friends.

"Your brother."

"No."

"No?"

"Family discussion is not on the menu tonight."

"Rena, you don't understand."

"I understand, but tonight, I want my husband to just be Sante and not a mob boss, or executive at a billionaire-dollar company."

"You're right."

"Thank you."

"Did you see the opening ceremony of ACE on TV?"

"A little, but you know they try to spin the narrative."

"At some point, you'll learn to ignore them."

"Anthony told you about the other day." I put my drink down on the table.

"He said you went to lunch with my mother and McKayla."

Sante's eyes lingered on me, and I felt like he knew that I took a call from my brother.

"The day started out good with me wanting to get McKayla out of the house."

"How is she doing with SJ?"

"She's doing great for a first-time mom. Did I tell you that your mom asked me about kids?"

"What was your answer?"

"Same answer I gave you. No kids, my career, and you are all I want."

Sante smiled and kissed the back of my palm.

"Tomorrow, what are you up to?"

"I've been in touch with Nikki, and we'll make a Face-Time call."

"Is she still in New York?"

"She was in Houston a month ago, then Paris."

"Sounds like you're on the right path to get your business going."

"Excited and nervous."

"It happens to the best of us, just enjoy the ride."

"Thank you again."

We clinked glasses, then went on to eat and laughed about SJ spitting up on Savio at night. Talk drifted to the bedroom after dinner, and he once again feasted on me until I couldn't think straight.

THE NEXT DAY, I stood outside my brother's office in deep thought. Should I walk through those doors and try to salvage our relationship? My mom still hadn't spoken to me after leaving multiple messages. I figured if Ted and I could come to terms, we could connect as a family with our mother.

"How are you, Rena?" Corinne, his secretary, asked.

"Doing good, Corinne. How are you?"

"Just fine. He's expecting you."

"Oh, great. Thanks."

"Tell him I'm heading to lunch if you don't mind."

Corrine placed her purse on her shoulder.

"Of course not. Have a good lunch."

Knock! Knock!

"Yeah, Corinne!"

I pushed the door open.

"It's me. Corinne told me to tell you she's going to lunch."

"Rena, come inside and have a seat."

"Thanks." I shut his door behind me.

"Thanks for meeting with me." Ted sat on the edge of his desk.

"You're my brother, I might not agree with everything, but I do love you."

"Happy to hear that, because I want you to forgive me and listen to me when I say Sante is no good for you."

"Ted, if you're going to try to break up my marriage, I won't stay."

"Why are you making this so difficult?"

"Difficult?"

"All your life, everything has been given to your spoiled ass. Now, because you married some rich guy, you think you're better than me."

"Ted, you've forgotten that we grew up with the same things. Our mother sacrificed for us both."

"This is how you repay her by being a bitch!"

"You haven't changed at all." I gathered my purse and rose from the chair. He grabbed me by the elbow before I tried to leave.

"You owe me."

"Let my arm go, Ted."

"Everything in my life is fucked up because of you."

"I'm the one who had to marry someone because of your gambling!"

The bathroom door opened, and Carmine stepped out.

"Hello, Rena."

I jerked out of Ted's hold.

"What is going on here?"

"You're going with Carmine."

"Ted, you've lost your mind."

"He's willing to ignore my debt if I let him have you."

I staggered backwards.

"Whaaat?" I stuttered in shock

"Ted, leave us alone."

"No, Ted, you can't do this."

"You should have listened to me the first time, Rena." Ted went to open the door and stopped at my words. Then he left the room.

"Wait! You're not leaving me alone with him."

"We're going to get to know each other better."

Carmine raised a palm to my cheek, and I smacked it away.

"Don't touch me!" I snapped, pushing him away.

He grabbed me by my arms, pushed me back on the desk, and gripped my chin.

"Get off me!" I tiredly went to scratch his face, as his hand went to my thigh and moved up to grope my left breast.

Knock! knock!

"Mr. Clark?"

Carmine moved back quickly, and I stood, grabbed my purse, and ran out of the office when Corinne interrupted.

"Rena, is everything—"

"Fine, Corinne. I need to go."

"What is it, Corinne?" Carmine asked when I walked out.

I ran to the elevator and hit the button as tears pooled in my eyes. I couldn't believe what almost happened and to think, my brother was willing to sacrifice me to save himself. Carmine came out of his office, and I ran down the hall to the exit doors. I shoved them open, put my back to them, and closed my eyes to gather a breath. Then my phone vibrated. Noticing my hands shaking and my nose running, I saw Sante's name scroll across and ignored the text message.

Sante: I have a surprise for you.

I put my phone back in my purse, left the building, and walked right into another disaster.

"Mrs. Calabresi! We have word your brother is meeting with a well-known mafia boss Carmine Colombo." A reporter stopped me from leaving the alleyway.

"Please leave me alone."

"What can you tell us about your brother's debt?"

I paused and looked at him.

"Don't you have better things to do than harass me?"

"Ma'am, your husband is a killer, and your brother has been shown to be stealing from his campaign."

"I don't know what you're talking about."

I stomped off and approached a taxi. I blew out a breath, gave the address to the driver, and slumped down in my seat.

TWENTY

The moonlight beamed down on her face, and she drew a deep, audible breath when I sank a wet finger through her core. I devoured her mouth, barely able to think clearly. A vein throbbed on her forehead. After the charity ball fiasco, Rena was distant, hurt from her brother's constant betrayal. Then yesterday. Ted sealed his fate. No longer would I stop Renato from extracting him from our lives. I stroked her cheek, and she leaned into my palm and raised her head to peer into my eyes.

"I need you, Sante."

"We need each other."

She let out an inward sigh of relief when my hand grazed against her juicy wetness. The desperate scent of her arousal kicked my heartbeat up a notch. I could almost hear the emotions choke at her when I lowered to face her hidden secrets between her thighs. Passionately kissing her inner thigh gently, I nibbled like a starving man as the boat swayed back and forth. Worshipping both thighs with a massage, I moved her hips gently at first, then faster when my tongue stiffened, licked, and sucked on her clit. Long strokes savored the slow burn, ached to not bury deep in her sex for my own pleasure. This was to serve her needs. Full tits called my name. I removed them from the strapless dress, stroked, and tweaked each nipple.

"Tell me how I can please you, baby."

"Fuck me."

"Slow or rough, baby."

"Rough; make the pain go away."

"Only thing that matters is us two."

My breath caressed her ear, peppered kisses along her neck, and nuzzled my neck in her shoulder. I clamped a hand around her neck, pulled back, and fucked her deep and long.

"Fuck! Mi Amore," I groaned, watching her body thrash underneath me.

"Oh God!" Rena screamed, reaching up to latch her lips to mine. Not long after, I switched our positions, letting her climb on top. I sucked on my thumb, rocked back and forth, and stared in my eyes with lust.

"Baby, please," I begged, smacking her on the ass.

"You please me so good, Sante." I was on fire for her.

"I want you always, Rena."

"You'll have me."

The moans from our lips encouraged us to close in on our peak. I tightened my arms around her waist, pulled her chest to chest, and flooded her walls with my seed. When she came home, I got a rundown from Viktor of her being at the hair salon, but the tracker said she was at Ted's office. I finally got her to talk to me, and I wanted to bring the entire force of my connections to throw him under the jail after what she told me.

"*I snuck out to see my brother.*"

"*What was the reason for the visit?*"

"*In my mind, we would reconnect as a family.*" She wiped her face.

"*What else happened?*"

"*He called me names and said I should leave you,*" she whispered. I let her gather her thoughts and didn't force her to speak.

"*I stood to leave, and Carmine was there.*"

I gritted my teeth and tried to control my temper.

"*It was like I didn't know who my brother was anymore.*"

"*Relax, baby.*"

"*He left me alone with Carmine.*"

"*Did he touch you?*"

"*He... he tried, but Corinne came in and interrupted him.*"

"Baby, we have to head back. Let's get cleaned up," I whispered in her ear. Her eyes fluttered open and rose off my chest. I covered her with my jacket, lifted her in my arms, and carried her to the bedroom as the captain started up the boat and headed back to the dock.

THREE DAYS later

Rena was hauled up in her new office, working on color schemes for her clothing line, and I decided to work from home to be near her. Lately, she'd had a rough time sleeping.

"Has she eaten yet?"

I closed the door behind McKayla and watched Savio talk on the phone behind her.

"We had breakfast."

"Perfect. She loves sweets, so I brought donuts and smoothies from her favorite place."

"Thanks for coming, McKayla."

"Anything for my friend.

"She's in the guest room turned office."

She chuckled and walked off.

"How is she really doing?" Savio angled toward me and ended his call.

"Better, in denial I think."

"Family and disappointment work like that."

"He's working like he's done nothing. Thinks I won't hurt him."

I slammed my fist into the couch.

"We have the place watched."

"As soon as I get my hands on him, he's dead."

"Carmine is still missing."

"Son of a bitch thinks he can get away with touching my wife."

"Hate to change the subject, but now the Serbian deal is coming up. We need to secure the trucks."

"I bought three more trucks."

"They'll be outfitted for specific jobs on this level."

"A few calls came in from other interested parties if we pull off the Serbians."

"I can deliver."

"If you take Ted out, there could be consequences."

"I have it all planned out. It can't come back on us."

We turned at the laughs that came from the hallway.

"You got her out of the room."

"Office." Rena stood on her tiptoes, pecked my lips, and gripped the back of my head.

"Sorry, office."

"Decided to watch some movies, do you mind?"

"No, have at it. I need to leave and handle some things with my brother."

"Thanks, babe."

"Anything else you need?"

"I have plans to go to New York," she blurted, and I froze.

"New York?"

"Just to visit Nikki and look into some business stuff."

"You're just telling me this now?"

"Slipped my mind."

"Are we arguing about this right now?"

"How long are you gone?"

"A few days, maybe a week."

"I can't go with you."

"That's fine. I can handle myself."

"You make it really hard to say no."

"I have Viktor. McKayla also offered me Anthony to be guards."

My eyes rose to McKayla, and Savio glared at her.

"She needs this, Sante," McKayla muttered, her eyes roaming toward Rena.

"Stay out of it, McKayla," Savio informed me.

"Calabresi men can drop the possessiveness for a second."

"It's in our blood. You're mine, and nothing will change that." Savio brushed a kiss over her cheek and followed me to the door to leave.

CHAPTER

TWENTY-ONE

RENA

McKayla and Savio visited with us yesterday for a few hours, then watched a movie before they had to leave and get back to the baby. I rolled over and rubbed Sante's chest as he slept with one arm wrapped around my waist; the other held my hand to his chest. We made love all night. He even took his time giving me a bath afterwards, and that provoked him to fuck me to sleep. I removed my hand, slid down his chest to roam over his length, and squeezed. His eyes popped open. I bit my lip as he pushed me on my back. My legs opened automatically for him.

"What time do you have to catch the flight?" He grinned at me.

"Agghh... I need to shower and be ready in an hour."

"Call me as soon as you make it there."

"I will."

Ring!

He groaned. I dropped my hand from his back and lifted my head to the nightstand.

184

"I have to take that."

"Whoever it is can wait. I need to make love to my wife."

"So... Ughhhh... demanding." He guided his dick in and slid out.

"Sshhh."

"They can wait," I mumbled, and we went for another round. Hours later, I rode in the car to the airport. I was supposed to leave in the early morning, but my over-sleeping and overprotective husband delayed my plans.

Ring!

I removed my phone from my pocket and saw the number to my brother's office.

"Hello?"

"Rena?"

"Yes."

"It's Corinne."

"Corinne, I don't know if you've heard, but I'm not dealing with my brother anymore."

"I understand. He left a note for you."

"Is he there?"

"No, he's coming in later."

"Is it important?"

"I'm not sure, but he wanted you to have it because it explains his decisions. I'm not sure what's going on though."

"Okay, I'll swing over and get it."

"Sounds great."

"Viktor, can you swing by my brother's office?"

"Boss said you're not supposed to be at his place."

"Viktor, he's not there. Besides, Corinne has a letter for me."

"Not sure."

"We have plenty of time. Just swing by, and she can bring it outside."

He turned at the light, headed to Ted's office, and I sat back with my head on the cushion. My mother still wasn't returning my calls. I hoped New York would change everything for me.

"We're here." Viktor honked the horn, and I rolled the window down.

"Here you go, Rena. I hope you two can make amends."

I grabbed the yellow envelope from her hands.

"Thanks."

The window went back up, and we headed to the airport. I dropped the envelope in my bag and decided to open it later when I got settled.

Ring!

"Are you here?" Nikki asked.

"No, almost at the airport."

"Can't wait for you to arrive. We'll have so much fun."

"No clubs, Nikki. This is a business trip."

"Completely understand. I know we're all about business this time."

"Good."

"I have a few meetings set up for you."

"Great."

"Why do you sound like your mind isn't on the trip."

"My brother made another attempt to get in touch with me."

"Leave Ted where he belongs, on an island by himself," Nikki responded, and I laughed. "He's in trouble with a lot of people. Stay out of it, Rena."

"Sante and McKayla already told me to, and I'd made up my mind as well."

"I love you, but you need to be okay with not having them in your corner anymore."

"That's the sad part. I have made my mind up. The Calabreses are the only ones who have been loyal."

"Happy for you."

"Thanks, Nikki. We just pulled up to the airport."

"Remember to come straight to my condo. If I'm not back home, the doorman will let you in."

"Okay, see you soon."

ONCE NIKKI CAME HOME last night, we had dinner and planned for me to meet a few people that could be potential support for my fashion line. We were at breakfast, and I slipped a piece of fruit in my mouth, listening to the designer of Ralph Lauren.

"Nikki told me you're doing the everyday women line," Maggie stated, and I nodded.

"Still in the early days; ideas are floating around."

"Do you know the amount of pieces you might need for the first show?"

"After I talked to Abigail in Paris, she said maybe an intimate small. Maybe a ten-item collection."

"That could be good. Find a few makeup and hair endorsements to sponsor gift bags."

"Exact idea I had," Nikki commented.

"If I can do anything, please let me know. Nikki, it's been a pleasure as usual." Maggie stood from the table and left.

"Breakfast is on me." Maggie left money on the table. "Your thoughts?"

"If we have more meetings like this, I'm onboard," I answered, sipping my coffee.

"Great. I know you're here for a limited time, but I have a few more meetings planned."

"Do you mind if we head back to the condo? I'm a little jetlag." I yawned and put my knife and fork down on the plate.

"You can't come to New York and be bored."

"I need a little nap. Then we can really see New York."

Nikki rose from her chair, and Viktor and Anthony approached, leading us out of the restaurant to our car. Climbing in after Nikki, I removed my phone from my purse to see if I had any messages.

"Focus on you. Leave Chicago problems back there."

"Hard to do that." I laid my hand on the side of my head.

We drove to her condo a few blocks away. Not even ten minutes later, he arrived, and Nikki stepped out. I trailed inside and listened to her talk about the latest guy she met at the club.

"He was cute, but he had no taste in clothes."

"You based having another date with his clothes?" I giggled at her statement.

"Horrible brown pants and maroon sweater, he looked like an old man." Nikki opened the door, and I laid my purse and phone down and picked up my bag to remove my sketchpad. The yellow envelope that Corinne gave me slid out and fell on the floor.

"What's that?" Nikki fixed her lip gloss.

"Something that Ted gave Corinne to give to me."

"He's trying to get back in your good graces. I have to make a few calls."

I bent down to pick up the envelope and peeled it open.

"Okay."

I flipped the contents over, and they fell on the couch.

CHAPTER

TWENTY-TWO

SANTE

The warning I gave him was ignored, and he thought I wouldn't do what I was about to do now. In the beginning, it wasn't love with Rena, but she became that person I would always protect and care for even if we weren't married. EJ sent over the intel on Ted's whereabouts since he tried to set my brother up to be killed and put me in jail. Rena was in New York at some fashion event. We arranged for Ted's car to break down on the street. From there, my men would bring him to me. I glanced at the time on the wall until I heard the garage doors open of the warehouse. The limo pulled in and stopped with my guards carrying Ted out with a black cloth over his head.

"Let me go! Do you know who I am?" he shouted, wrangling to get out of their hold.

"Let him go."

He froze at my voice as they removed the mask from his head.

"Sante..." he stuttered, trying to back up and run. My

190

men caught him and pushed him forward as he stumbled.

"Ted, you've disappointed me."

Ted looked around the room, and my men stood on both sides of him. This decision wasn't haphazard but to have peace. His secretary usually texted him the agenda for the next day, so we downloaded an app to clone her number, and she'd get a response without knowing it wasn't him.

"Wait, you can't do this."

"Ted, what do you think is going to happen here?"

"Listen, I can help you get Carmine. It won't be an issue."

"Oh, I already have plans for him."

Ted took off running into the side of the building with an exit sign, I cut my men off to stop.

"He's not going anywhere."

After not being able to open the door, he panicked, slamming his hand and shouting to get someone to come.

"Ted, it's time."

He shook his head and fell to the ground. I stalked over to him, dropped down low, and lifted his head up by my gun.

"All you had to do was keep quiet."

"Please, I'll give you whatever you want."

"I have it all, Teddy boy." I tapped his chin lightly.

"We can make a deal," he pleaded. I grasped him by the collar, dragged him over to the ropes, and motioned to my men to tie him up.

"What is this? Hold up, Sante. Please... no!" he screamed, hanging up in the middle of the room.

"Strip him."

They removed his jacket, shoes, and pants, leaving him only in his boxers. My guard stepped over and poured gasoline all over his body. He wiggled and choked from it getting in his mouth.

"This is for you betraying me."

I pulled out a cigar and lighter from my pocket and stood back as a soldier punched him in the stomach.

"No! Stop, I'll do anything."

I blew smoke from my lips, then nose, and laid the cigar across his chin, dug it into his jaw.

"Ahh!!!"

Finishing off the cigar, I dropped it on the ground and twisted it under my shoe to put it out.

"Pass me the knife." One of my men handed the long butcher knife to me, and I touched the tip and smirked.

"I usually would leave this to Renato, so he's going to be pissed." I grinned. Ted tried to move backwards, then to the left and right side, away from the knife as I held it in my hand.

Touching it against his chest, I pushed it forcefully into his skin to draw blood and listened to him scream, with tears and snot falling down his face.

"You... can't... get away with this," he muttered through tears.

I walked behind him and dragged the knife from the bottom of his back up to his neck, and he cried in pain. He trembled against the pain as I lit another cigar and watched him bleed out, feeling relief and content.

"I need... help," he mumbled. I ignored him and pushed the cigar in his wounds.

"Help won't come this time."

"Police will catch you. Rena won't let you get away with this."

"Say goodbye, Ted." I flicked the cigar on him, and he was engulfed in flames. We spun and stalked out of the warehouse, as they continued pouring gasoline on the building. I slid in the car, and we pulled a distance away as the building went up in flames.

"Has she texted?" I asked. Elio held up his phone.

"In five more minutes, we should be good," he replied.

The car headed down the road, heading to the freeway. Rena's flight was supposed to come in tomorrow, and I planned to have a driver pick her up from the airport.

Buzz!

"This is her." Elio typed on his cell phone.

"What did you say?"

"Cancel, I have a prior engagement," he read the statement.

"Good. By the time he doesn't show, they'll think he's off to Fiji and skipped out on his duties."

"And Rena."

"What about her?"

"How are you going to handle it if she finds out?"

"It was either him or you."

"She's your wife, Sante."

"Give me a break, Elio. He was going to kill you and put me in jail."

"I'm not disputing you, but things like this can backfire."

"Worry about your relationship with Cora," I snapped and pulled my phone out of my pocket to see if Rena had texted me. The ride would be another twenty minutes before we made it home, and I needed rest.

"I'm sorry for snapping," I spoke and placed my phone in my pocket.

"You're protecting your family, I understand."

"She'll need to understand."

"All we can hope is that the truth will come out."

Twenty minutes later, we arrived. I jumped out, not waiting for someone to open the door.

"Call me tomorrow so we can work out the details on Carmine."

"I will." I shook hands with him and strolled to the elevator and stepped on. I stood in the back corner as the elevator doors closed and ran a hand down my face, briefly closing my eyes.

"*Please, she'll never forgive you for this!*" My eyes popped up at the memory of Ted's final words.

~

Ring! Ring!

Next morning, I groaned in bed, remembering the nightmare of Ted's body turning into Rena's as it went up in flames. I'd killed plenty of people but never had any regrets until now. I hit the alarm clock, stretched my arms in bed, and sat up against the headboard. Her bags weren't near the bed, and I didn't hear anyone come inside. I checked my cell but didn't have any missed calls.

"It's almost ten in the morning," I mumbled to myself. Her flight was supposed to come in at eight a.m. I dialed her number, and it went straight to voicemail, so I hung up and tried it again.

"You've reached Rena Clark. Please leave a message at the beep."

Ring!

Renato's name flashed across my screen, and I hurriedly answered.

"You talk to Rena?" he asked, my ears perked up at his question.

"No, why?"

"I need you to meet me at the family home."

"Why?"

"Because I don't need you going off and doing something stupid."

"What are you talking about, Renato?"

"Just meet us at the house."

I jumped out of bed, dialed Rena's number again, and this time it said the number had been disconnected. I pulled it away from my ear and wondered if Carmine had gotten to her again. Turning on the shower, I picked up my toothbrush and waited for the water to get hot. Still pissed at Rena's phone being disconnected, I called Renato back as I stalked in the bathroom.

"Have you left the house?"

"Getting dressed now, but Rena's phone is off."

With a heavy sigh, panic swept through my body.

"Sante, I need you to wait for me to get there."

"Why? Renato, tell me what's going on with my wife!"

"She's gone."

I stumbled back on the bed.

"What?"

"Well, as far as we know, McKayla is the only one she is talking to right now."

"What's happened?"

"She knows about you killing Ted."

In disbelief, I repeatedly blinked my eyes.

"How?"

"Ted."

It was like a knot in my stomach.

"Ted is dead, Renato."

"The secretary received a package, and she forwarded it to Rena. I guess Ted had it planned out if something happened to him, you were the cause."

"Fuck!" I shouted, swiped my arm across the dresser, and knocked everything on the floor.

"All we know is that Rena is still in New York."

"What about the men that I had with her?"

"She dodged them."

"Renato, I want my wife found now."

"I'm working on that now, but you need to get over here because we still have Carmine to deal with."

"Son of bitch planned this whole thing out."

"We'll find her." His tone was a little odd when he talked about finding her.

"What about the secretary?"

"She's in hiding, but we've put a few things in motion."

"Don't kill her."

"What if she—"

"No, we have enough noise around our names right now."

"You sure about that."

"If we have to pay her off, do that but don't kill her."

"All right."

"I'm heading to Savio's now to talk to McKayla."

"You know Savio won't let you talk to her right now."

"I need to find my wife."

"I'll meet you there. I can see you both killing each other," he grumbled and ended the call. I ran to my dresser, picked up a pair of boxers, jeans, and shirt to change into, while I dialed soldiers I had in New York.

"Mr. Calabresi." He sounded out of breath.

"Where are you?"

I snatched my keys off the table, as well as my wallet and jacket to leave, hopping on the elevator. I checked my watch and hit the lobby button as the doors closed.

"I'm outside the hotel Mrs. Calabresi was staying at."

"Keep me updated. I'm sending Nikki's address to you now."

"Got it, boss."

"If you see her, call me."

"Sure, boss."

The door opened, and my driver stood waiting as I climbed the car. He shut the door behind me.

"To Savio's place."

"Yes, sir, Mr. Calabresi."

I underestimated Ted and his conniving nature, but I wouldn't let him come up here and fuck up my marriage and happiness. The limo turned off the freeway I'd normally stay on when heading to Savio's home. Alarms went off in my head.

"This isn't the turn, Danny."

He didn't answer.

"Danny."

The partition dropped down, and my eyes rose in shock at Carmine sitting in the passenger seat with Danny next to him. I'd known Danny for over five years as my driver, and this betrayal would not be tolerated by my family.

"Surprised?"

I forgot my gun and didn't do anything to defend

myself. I cursed under my breath as he held a gun up to my face.

"You know, I figured you thought you were better than me, especially with that hot wife of yours."

"Shut the fuck up about my wife."

"She's a sweet, little, feisty thing I'd like to knock down once or twice." He grinned, holding a photo up of Rena and Nikki together. I leaned over the seat to punch him, and he pushed the partition back up. The car stopped on a deserted street, and the door opened with a gun pointed at my face.

"I'll make this easy for you. Come out of the car slowly," Carmine explained, standing next to his bodyguard. As I climbed out, he raised his hand with the gun and knocked me on the back of the head.

"Shit!" I groaned and fell to my knees.

"Fucking pussy, get up, boss! That's what you are, right?" Carmine taunted, raising his leg and kicking me in the stomach.

"Fuck!" I spat out blood, rolling onto my back.

"Pick him up and bring him to the car."

"What are you going to do to him, boss?"

"We'll show him how a real boss does things to an enemy." He chuckled, pushing me forward toward the other car. As they shoved me inside, I glanced back at Danny and saw a bullet pierce him between the eyes.

"Can't have any loose ends," Carmine muttered, sliding into the passenger side. The dodger pulled off as the limos stayed behind with a body lying on the ground. I should have waited for Renato to pick me up, but I didn't think Carmine would be this fast in retaliation. He must have found out about Ted's death and knew we were coming for him next.

"Unlike how you did Maurizio, I'll give you a choice in how you die."

"If I die, the entire force of the clan will come for you."

"You hear this, Rodrigo? The whole force of the Calabresi Clan."

"I hear it, boss," Rodrigo replied, continuing to drive.

"What you fail to realize, Sante, is that I don't have anything holding hostage of my heart like you do."

My eyes dipped low, as I bit into my bottom lip.

"See, that's it. You have a family, a wife."

"You come near my father, and I'll destroy you."

"Fuck the Calabreses!" he shouted, as we arrived at ACE Trucking.

"What are you doing here?"

"You're going to sign over the company to me." He opened the door, came around to my side, and held the gun at his waist.

"Come on."

"I'm not signing anything to you."

"Yes, you are, or your wife is going to die."

"What did you do to her?" I charged at him. The guard punched me in the side of the stomach.

"Nothing yet, but my men are working on finding her and Nikki." He smirked, squeezing my chin hard.

"Leave her out of this."

"Not until I have everything."

CHAPTER
TWENTY-THREE

RENA

few hours before in New York

All day, it played over and over in my mind. A moving picture that I didn't want to be a part of but couldn't escape, no matter how many times I tried. I was stuck in place looking at pictures of my brother being pulled from his office by Sante's bodyguard. Now I heard on the news that he was missing and no ransom money had been brought up. He'd told me that I couldn't trust Sante, and I argued that he was wrong and to give him a chance to get to know the family. My mother was heartbroken and still waiting on hope he'd come home. The package she forwarded in the mail was addressed to my brother, stating that if something happened to him, it was the Calabreses' fault and to go to the police. Here I was, standing here contemplating whether to turn in my husband or not.

"What have you decided?"

"I don't know, Nikki."

I stood from the chair, walked to the kitchen, and

poured a cup of coffee. I had meetings planned for this week but canceled everything when I got the news.

"If this was you, how would you handle things?"

"I can't answer that for you, babe."

"This should be the happiest time for me, but I'm dealing with my brother possibly dead and my husband being responsible."

"Don't blame yourself."

I wiped the tears that rolled down my cheeks.

"He was my brother, even though we had problems. Does that make me crazy for still loving Sante?"

"No, of course not. Have you talked to your mom?"

"No, she was supposed to call me when she heard anything."

"Are you flying back home?"

"No."

"Rena," she sighed, rubbing along my back.

"I just need to think and if I'm in Chicago, I wouldn't have any space to figure things out."

"I understand, but you can't run away from your problems."

"Says the girl who lives in one city every other month." I giggled and sat in front of my laptop and searched on social media for any updates.

"Has McKayla called you?"

"No, and I can't worry about her with my problems."

"She's your best friend."

"Yeah, but a new baby and a crazy husband who I'd rather not deal with for now."

"No news is good news, right?"

"I guess."

"Then get to figuring out the fashion show details to keep your mind on something else."

"Maybe I should call the police or his office to get an update."

"They said they'll call if something changes. Your brother's been into some crazy shit, Rena. Be honest with yourself."

Nikki was right, and he'd embezzled from his own campaign and gambled himself into debt. A woman even popped up in an interview saying he assaulting her. This was the brother I grew up with. Yes, he was an asshole, but to turn into a money-hungry, gambling criminal was something I couldn't swallow.

"Do you have the printouts of the seating arrangement?"

At this moment and time, I needed to focus on what I could control, and that was my business and the fashion show I wanted to put together with my debut looks.

"Here you go." Nikki leaned over the table and pulled up the sketchbook I'd started playing around with some ideas.

"Thinking ten looks, something small and intimate."

Ring!

I glanced down at my phone ringing and noticed Sante calling me.

"Are you going to answer?"

"No, I can't talk to him right now."

"He's going to get worried."

"Let him. It's time I start making him sweat a little."

Ring!

"Okay, do you have a theme in mind?"

"Everyday woman, classic, clean pieces."

"We could rent out an intimate space, so we're not overwhelmed."

"That's a good idea."

"I'll start to call around."

"Set up auditions for models."

"Where are you planning to have the event?"

"Here."

"In New York?"

I nodded, typing notes on my iPad.

"Are you planning to stay here the whole time?"

"I'll go back to visit my mom, but then come back up here right after."

"Drowning yourself in work won't make things go away."

"Can you please not lecture me, Nikki?"

"As your friend and McKayla's substitute, I have to remind you of what's important."

"My work is what's important at the moment, so try to keep that in mind please." I rose from the couch, picked up the cup, and headed to the kitchen to refill my coffee. I didn't like to snap at my friends, but she wasn't helping the situation any better.

"Have you eaten anything today?"

Ring!

My head moved to my phone ringing, and I saw my mother's name across the screen and answered.

"Hey, Mom."

"They're saying he's dead, Rena!" The tears rolled down my cheeks as she cried out in pain.

"Do they know what happened?"

"No, his cell phone was traced to some deserted warehouse. When they went there, it was burned down." With a hand on my mouth, I gasped in shock, angry with resentment.

"Let me call you back."

"Rena, please be careful. We don't know who did this."

I know full well, but I couldn't tell her that.

"I love you." I ended the call and dialed Savio's number.

"Hello." Groggily, he answered.

"Your family did this, and I'll never forgive him or you. The only thing I ask is to not keep McKayla from me."

"Rena?" he probed.

"You knew, didn't you?"

"What is this about?"

"Stop playing dumb, Savio!" I shouted.

"Look, let me explain."

"So, you can lie!"

"He had to make a decision."

"That destroys my family."

"We're your family too."

"Who is that, Savio?" I heard McKayla's voice.

"Does she know?"

"Where are you? Come talk to us in person."

"Does McKayla know that your brother killed my brother?"

"Rena, listen."

"Answer the question goddamnit!"

The phone was silent for a few minutes.

"No, she'd just had a baby. She doesn't need to know any of this, and I expect you to keep it to yourself."

I laughed in astonishment at the arrogance.

"Yeah, we wouldn't want to show the monster that lies in the Calabresi men."

～

PRESENT TIME

After the other day with Savio and my mother, I shut everyone off and changed my number. I didn't need the constant barrage of calls or McKayla worrying about me. I didn't know what my life was now. Without a father growing up, when the brother you'd looked up to suddenly became someone you'd never met, it stung like an arrow through the heart.

The flight back from New York wasn't too bad, and I held up well without breaking down. I still hadn't taken a call from my husband and refused anyone else from reaching out except McKayla or my mother. I parked the car and grabbed my bag out of the backseat. I slid my purse on my shoulder and talked to Nikki on the phone as I headed up to the door of my mother's house.

"Do you need me to fly out there?"

"No. Stay there and focus on canceling the vendors."

"I hate this has happened to your family, Rena."

I stepped in the house and saw flowers lined up on the wall near the foyer. I placed my bag on the floor and headed to the living room where I heard voices.

"Let me call you back." As soon as I clicked the end button on the phone, I removed my shades. Across the room, my mother was embracing her neighbor who lived two houses down. She was a widow unlike my mom, who'd been single for the last twenty years.

"Mom."

She stepped out of her hold, swung her head, and extended a hand to me.

"Rena baby, it's true."

"Yes."

"How are you, Rena?" Ms. Rachel embraced me.

"Doing as best as I can, Ms. Rachel."

"I told your mother I cooked dinner, so if you're hungry, I have food in the kitchen."

"Maybe later."

"Rachel, do you mind if we talk alone for a second?" Mother probed.

"Yes, let me check on the sandwiches."

Ms. Rachel ran a hand over my mom's palm.

Mother locked arms with me and pulled me to the couch.

"He wasn't the most loved by the world, but he was my son."

"I remember when we were kids, I used to force him to let me ride on his back." I chortled, leaning my head on her shoulder.

"Raising you two was hard, but I made it my mission for you two to become successful."

"I'm grateful for you."

"Oh baby, I'm grateful for you too, baby."

Ring!

"Ugh, let me answer this. It's probably Nikki. She's trying to get my vendors canceled. I told everyone I had a family emergency and to not contact me."

"I'll give you some privacy." She stood and walked out of the room.

"Hello." I rubbed my temples.

"Rena, it's Elio."

"Elio, I told your brother to not contact me."

"He's missing."

I gasped, jumping up in shock.

"What?"

"He's missing. He never arrived at Savio's."

"Missing," I repeated, low to myself.

"I'm sending some men to bring you to Savio's house?"

"Elio…"

"Either you come, or we have people guarding your mother's home, which brings an audience."

"All right, I'll go."

"He only did it to protect you," Elio said, and I heard the phone click.

Honk!

I walked over to the window, slid the curtain back, and saw a car outside.

"This is a joke. He never gave me the option to not come." I marched around to the front door, snatched it open, and saw Renato standing with the door open.

"Rena, what's going on?" Mom probed.

"I'll be back. Don't worry." I kissed her cheek, walked toward Renato, and stopped before his face.

"He would kill me if I didn't keep you protected." Renato directed me inside after he explained what he was doing.

"Where was he last spotted?" The door closed shut.

"Coming to Savio's house." Renato got in the front passenger seat, and the car drove off.

"Did you convince him to kill my brother?"

They went silent, and the driver looked over at him.

"Come on, keep it real with me, Renato."

"How honest do you want me to be?"

"Truthful."

"Your brother was in a lot of debt and tried to put my brother in jail. I never give second chances."

"He's my family."

"We all have a burden to bear."

The driver rotated left out of the cul de sac to the stop

sign, then pulled onto the main street. I stared out the window and watched the moving cars. I looked down at my empty ring finger, wondering if Sante at any moment had doubts before he made the decision on my brother. Eventually, we arrived, and Renato opened the door for me. I trailed behind, and the door opened to McKayla holding the baby. She circled an arm around my neck, and I kissed her cheek, then little Savio Jr.

"You look like you haven't slept in days."

"I haven't."

"Come in. Adelina has cooked."

"Everyone's here?" I paused at the door.

"Yeah, soon as word got out that Sante was missing."

"Maybe I should go."

"Rena! Oh, thank God you're safe." Adelina pulled me in a tight embrace.

"Hi Adelina." Sorrow filled her voice, and I tried to avoid this moment, because I cared about his parents very much. But their son went too far, and I needed to distance myself from this family as fast as possible.

"Rena, my dear, I'm happy to see you." His father slipped his arm around me.

"Mr. and Mrs. Calabresi, sorry to hear about all this. Have you heard anything?"

"Our men are looking into his last known location."

"Danny was found dead in the limo," Renato spoke, staring at his phone.

"Did they say where?" Elio asked, trailing him to the door.

"A half mile from his condo," Renato answered.

"I'm going with you," their father expressed.

"No, you should stay here." Savio came into the room and grabbed Savio Jr. from McKayla's arms. He was a cute butterball with his father's eyes, black curly hair, and striking eyes that looked deep into your soul.

"We'll keep in touch once we get word," Renato muttered and continued to leave the house.

"Come sit down and tell me what's happening, Rena," McKayla said, patting the seat next to her. I ran a hand through my hair, gathering up the strength to go into details of the past few days.

TWENTY-FOUR

SANTE

lick!

Carmine pressed the gun in front of my face, as blood seeped out the corner of my mouth, and sweat dripped down my face as my chest heaved up and down. He'd dragged me into the loading dock of ACE Trucking and demanded I sign everything over to him. Something in him gave him the idea that he could get away with trying to kill an underboss of another family. I spat on the ground, leaned my head up, and stared around the room with one swollen eye. Carmine seethed with fury, and I grinned. He took the back of the handle on the gun and hit me on the head, and I dropped down on the ground. His men stood around the room holding AK 47s. I observed his movements as he rambled off to himself.

"How much longer will you last?" Carmine spun around to me.

"Either you can leave now, or my brothers will kill you."

"Your brothers are next on my list."

"That'll never happen," I argued, watching the confidence leave his face.

"Sign over the company, and I'll think about letting your wife live."

The sound of him touching my wife caused me to lean up and charge at him, but his men hit me on the back of the leg between my knee and calf.

"Arghhh! I fell to the ground and pulled my leg up to my chest.

"Big bad Sante can't handle a little pain."

"Fuck you, Carmine."

"Wait until I get the approval from the other families."

"They'll never betray my father."

"You got balls; I can admit that."

"Go ahead and kill me. I'm not giving you anything."

"I guess I better fulfill your wish." He raised the gun up and aimed at me. I waited for everything to go black, as pictures of Rena poured in my mind.

Rattata!!! Pop!!

I popped my eyes open and saw Carmine dead on the ground with his eyes open. I jerked my head to the right and saw Renato and Elio with our soldiers taking out each of Carmine's men. I crawled over for cover behind a stack of crates and looked to see if I could pick up anything to protect myself.

"Sante!" Where are you?" Renato shouted, running up to a guy and punching him in the face.

"Here!" I replied. A guy tried to come behind me to drag me out, but I smacked the gun away, landing on top of him, and punched him in the chest.

"Renato, over here!" I growled, gripped his hair, and smashed his head into the ground.

"Renato, duck!" I yelled, sending a shot to the bastard.

Elio and Renato ran over to me, and I dropped the gun down to my side.

"You hurt?" Elio studied me over.

"A little sore. Just get me home."

"We'll call the doctor to meet us there."

"Lean on my shoulder," Elio stated.

"I'm going to secure the building. A car will take you back," Renato explained, and I nodded. We strolled out of the building to the cars lined up.

"Sante, you all right?"

Elio tapped me on the cheek.

"Get... mee..." I slurred my words, fell to the ground, and felt my eyes roll to the back of my head.

~

"Doctor, is he going to be all right?"

"He needs his rest; he's pretty banged up."

"He passed out twice." I heard Elio's voice and a beeping noise. My head was so foggy.

"But no major damage, right?" The sound of my mother's voice caused a shock to my heart.

"A few bruises, swollen eye. In time with rest, he'll be back to normal."

My eyes slowly blinked open. The first person I saw was my mother sitting on the side of the bed.

"Where am I?" My voice came out raspy. I tried to raise my hand to rub my forehead, but it was connected to a monitor.

"You're with us, Sante, at the family home." Mom soothingly raised her hand to my cheek with the back of her palm.

"Where's Renato and Elio?" I asked, trying to get out of bed. She pushed me down.

"They're fine, son. Stay down, you need your rest."

The demand in my father's voice reminded me of when I was younger, and he went off on different missions while we had to stay home in worry.

"Did you get Carmine? What about the other families?" I rambled off questions, and my mother handed me a cup of water.

"No business talk. You need to rest," Mom answered.

"Where's Rena?"

Their eyes connected, and I wondered what they were hiding and if Rena was okay.

"Get some rest. I'll have food brought up," Mom said.

"No, tell me where's Rena. I need to know if my wife is okay."

"Sante, please calm down."

"Did something happen to her? Tell me, Papa!" I hurt the side of my stomach when I tried to get up again. I ran my hand over the banged stomach.

"We'll talk once you've rested. Take these." Mom handed me two pills, and I shook my head.

"I don't need anything. Just leave me alone."

Knock! Knock!"

"I heard shouting and figured he was up." Vincenzo pushed the door further open and approached the bed. He stretched down and tapped my leg.

"What the hell were you thinking?" he quipped.

"I wasn't."

"We'll leave you alone and have food sent up." Mom kissed me on the cheek and walked out with my father.

"Where's everyone?"

"Renato and Elio are downstairs. Cora's helping her mom cook food."

"Rena." I darted my eyes up to a look of avoidance on his face.

"I've never lied to you, Sante. She doesn't want to see you right now."

"What? Why?"

"It's all over the news about Ted Clark being killed."

"So?"

"The bastard sent information that implicated you."

"How?"

"He mailed a letter and said if something happened to him, it would be your fault."

"To look at me as the first suspect?"

"It didn't help that she received pictures of him with our men carrying him out against his will."

Fuck!"

"Yeah, just give her a little space for right now."

"Where is she now?"

"At McKayla's."

"What about Ted's secretary?"

"Savio gave her a nice little raise to keep her mouth shut."

"I need to go talk to her." I tossed the covers to the side, moved to the edge of the bed. The quick movements took more energy than I had, and I fumbled back on the bed in dizziness.

"Bro, you need to eat and rest."

"How long have I been here?"

"Two days asleep."

"Two days!" I yelled.

"No one thought I should know that my wife left me?"

"The doctors said you were banged up badly and didn't need any stress."

I motioned him away and sat back under the cover.

"You're right. I need to just relax."

"Maybe you rushed into this thing with Rena too fast."

"I don't need a lecture from my little brother."

"Everything all right in here?" I looked behind my little brother at Renato.

"He's trying to leave to see Rena." Vincenzo ratted me out.

"The doctor mentioned you need to rest. Carmine did a number on you."

"Fuck that pussy."

"I agree, but if you want to get your wife back, you need to gain your strength."

"She's not leaving me."

"She's making plans to move back to New York."

I gnawed on my jaw and tightened my fists at his remark.

"Who told you that?"

"I overheard her talking to McKayla."

"Let me see your phone."

"Why do you call and get yourself even more upset?"

"Either give me your phone, or I'll take it."

"Come and try," Renato taunted, grinning mischievously with both arms lined up on his chest as he stood against the wall.

"Fuck you," I snapped, settling back in the bed and closing my eyes.

"The next time you think about going after a senator, rethink your decision," Renato mentioned.

"Have our lawyers worked everything out?"

"We're in the clear, but we need to make sure ACE is on the straight and narrow for a little while."

"Our next big shipment is supposed to go out in a few weeks."

"It will, but after that, we need to lay low."

"Calabresi Inc. is a stakeholder in ACE," Vincenzo groaned, his eyes boring in me.

"I'm with little bro. We can't have our legitimate business get caught up."

I blew out a breath and rubbed my eyes.

"You're right. After the load goes through, we'll keep any deals out for at least three months."

"The lawyer made a statement on your behalf to clear your name."

"What did he say?"

"Ted Clark's abduction and killing had nothing to do with you."

"How did he pull that off?"

Next time, we'd cover our tracks more to leave no loose ends.

"Basically, Ted was in debt to so many criminal organizations, they couldn't pin it on you."

"And what else?"

"A sum of ten million dollars was given unanimously from his defrauded campaign. Our hands are clean."

"Money."

"It makes everything right in the world." Renato pushed off the wall and whirled to leave my room.

"Hey, are you going to be good?" Vincenzo begged.

"Tell Mom to bring the food up. I need to be alone for a while."

He nodded and slapped hands with me.

"Glad you're home."

"Me too."

I stared at Vincenzo's back as he followed Renato, then sat in thought for a few minutes of the decisions I'd made and how my life had spun out. I didn't regret a lot of these, but hurting my wife was the one I'd never forgive myself for until I got her back in my arms.

A MONTH LATER, I was back to being my old self, building my strength up from working out at the gym, boxing, and swimming laps in the pool at my parents' home. I hadn't gone home because I knew she wasn't there, and the smell of her surrounded everything in our condo. I remembered the last argument when I tried to see her at Savio's house.

"Sante, she doesn't want to talk to you right now." McKayla stood at the door, holding my nephew. Savio was out with my brothers and told me not to upset his wife, but she was the only one who could talk some sense into Rena. McKayla knew, based on her past with Savio, the deep need to only want that one person who hurt you.

"*McKayla, tell her I'm not leaving until she talks to me.*"

"*She needs space; you do as well.*"

"*Would he be here if you gave space to Savio?*" I rubbed Savio Jr.'s little hand.

"*That's not fair, Sante. You killed her brother,*" she harshly whispered.

"*It had to be done. He was planning to hurt her.*"

"*All the more reason you should have included her in the decision.*"

"*That's not how the business is run.*"

"Please get over this keeping wives in the dark."

"McKayla."

She held a hand up, cutting me off.

"The difference between Savio and our situation is that I knew the decisions behind our marriage."

"She knew this wasn't a fairy tale."

"But you kept her sheltered like a princess. You can't have it both ways whether she's all in or out."

I dropped my head at her statement.

"I'll be back, but I'm not giving up."

"I hope not. You two belong together."

"Thanks, McKayla."

"Go home. Work on getting in her good graces."

I set the gloves down on the floor, picked up the bottle of water, and took a sip, blowing out my breath.

Knock! Knock!

"It's open."

"I hope you're not working too hard." Mom stood at the entrance.

"It helps me relax."

"Relaxing is good."

"You usually don't come in here."

I slid the gloves back on my hands, grabbed the towel, and wiped the sweat down my naked chest.

"I had to check on you and see how you're doing."

"You ready for me to leave your house?" I joked.

She giggled and waved me off.

"Some days, I wish all my boys were little again and moved back home."

"Papa would strangle us," I teased, and she laughed.

"True. He likes retirement and his peace with just the two of us."

"Did McKayla call you to check up on me?"

Her eyebrows drew into slits.

"No, why would you ask that?"

"Because I've been calling their house every day asking for Rena."

"Oh, well, Savio said he's going to change their number."

Our laughter erupted at her statement.

"He was the main one drowning his sorrows when McKayla broke up with him."

"Please don't remind your brother of that time."

My hands went up, and I leaned my right side forward into a fighting stance before punching the heavy weight bag hanging from the wall.

"Rena is here."

I froze in position and deviated to her.

"What did you say?"

"Rena is in the living room."

"Why? Is she all right?"

"She's fine physically. Mentally and emotionally, I'm not sure."

"I need to see her." I started to remove the gloves from my hands.

She blocked me from leaving the gym.

"Sante, before you go out there, I want to say something."

"What?" My left brow hiked in annoyance.

"No matter what she tells you, support her decision."

"What do you mean? Did she tell you something?"

"I love Rena and McKayla like daughters. I keep our conversation close to my heart, but at the end of the day, I'm a woman like them."

"Madre."

"Son, you need to listen."

I sighed, looking into her eyes for a few moments, then nodded.

"I won't go on a killing spree like Savio." I smirked, and she cupped my shoulder.

"Good, because our family name has been run through the mud enough."

I chuckled and wrapped an arm around her shoulder. She pushed me off as we left the gym.

"Go shower."

"What? I smell good." I lifted my arm to smell myself and watched her pinch her nose.

"For everyone's sake, go shower first."

"Fine, can I have a hug?" I stretched out to hug her, and she pushed me back.

I raced up to my bedroom and removed the gloves. The image of Rena naked on her knees and her pregnant belly occupied my mind, and I stroked the tip of my dick until my cum spurted out on the ground. Turning the shower off, I stepped out, dried off, and picked out slacks and shirt to throw on. Hurrying downstairs, I saw her laughing while sitting with my mother and father. I cleared my throat, and all attention went to me.

TWENTY-FIVE

RENA

His presence was felt even before I heard the voice as he stepped in the room. Our energy was dangerous, explosive, unpredictable, all the more reason I shouldn't be here right after what he'd done. People would question my loyalty and beliefs. Hell, I'd questioned myself plenty of times, but I had questions, and I needed answers. His parents had been supportive along, with Savio surprisingly and McKayla with letting me stay at their home for the past week. I didn't know he was still staying at his parents' home the whole time until he'd stepped in to talk to me.

"We'll give you some privacy." His father stood to leave, along with his mother.

"Thank you again, Mr. and Mrs. Calabresi."

"Call us for anything, Rena," his mom suggested.

A smile spread across my face, and we hugged again.

"I will."

They left us alone, and I felt my resolve going down.

"You wanted to talk." His brows creased together in anger as he took a step forward, and I moved back.

"How are you feeling?"

"Fine, but you know that already."

Our eyes met, and I saw the heaviness of our separation on his face.

"What were his last words?"

"Rena..." He rubbed a hand across the back of his neck.

"Tell me."

"You don't need to know."

"Tell me!" I shouted, and he stretched out to grab me, I held a hand up to block him from moving forward.

"Stay there."

"You're my wife."

"You were my husband."

At my words, his cheeks turned red in a flash of concern.

"Were your husband?" He repeated my words.

I stepped over to the mantel and grabbed the picture of him and his family together at Christmas.

"The first time I saw you, I knew you were trouble. Savio was the big-time boss, but you..." I pointed at him.

"Rena, I love you."

"You're underhanded, cutthroat, take whatever you want."

"It was business," he hissed.

"My life shouldn't be destroyed for your business."

"That is not what I mean."

"Then tell me... husband," I snapped and put the picture frame back down.

"Ted plotted with Carmine to have you assaulted and killed."

"I know."

"Then you know as your husband, I would do anything to protect you."

"There's ways to protect me without destroying my family!" I sputtered, pushing at his chest when he closed the space between us.

"No, don't touch me."

He cupped my chin, lifted my face up, and crashed his lips to me.

"Mhmmmmm...."

His arms went around my waist, and he ran a hand up and down my back.

"No, you need to explain to me why that was the only choice." I shoved him backwards, and he released his hold.

"His actions led to a lot of things being revealed about the five families. On top of that, you were being used as a pawn. I couldn't let him get away with hurting you."

"All of your connections, and this is what you choose to do. My mom couldn't even bury her child."

"I apologize for that."

"I can't pretend this doesn't hurt even if he wouldn't have given me the same courtesy."

"Baby."

"Give me space, Sante."

"No."

"I'm going to New York for a few weeks."

"No."

"Sante, our marriage was based on lies and corruption. You didn't marry me for love."

"Do you really believe that?"

"It was arranged so you can get money and be the top mafia family or whatever the hell you do!" I moved around him with my back to him.

"What I believe and know is that I love you, and the marriage was arranged, but I didn't do it as a way to save you."

Quickly, I wheeled around to face him.

"What are you saying?"

"Women would come and go, but marriage was not something I wanted until you."

"Meaning?"

"Ted's involvement came later. I blackmailed him, but we didn't get his background until later."

"So..."

"Carmine was never after you until he got word about our marriage. It was me he was after."

"So, you lied to marry me."

"Everytime you came into my presence when you lived with me during the kidnapping, I wanted to tell you how much happiness and stability you brought to my life."

"You forced me to live with you."

"At first, it was supposed to be temporary. Savio remarked I could let you go, but I loved having you around. Your fiery red hair, the fussy way you'd wake in the morning if you didn't have coffee first." He chuckled.

"What about all those times you tried to get rid of my dates?"

His eyes rolled, and I smiled at the way he appeared agitated by the thought of me dating.

"You loved flirting in front of my face or leaving all of your clothes and makeup scattered everywhere."

"I was a single woman, Sante."

"You were mine then. You just needed a little push, and you're mine now."

He pulled me into his chest and stared into my eyes. I brushed his lips across my cheek and down my neck.

"How would you like me to stay with you after what you did?"

"Fuck what other people think or say," he growled, sinking his face into my neck.

"This would destroy my mother. She's all I have."

"We can talk to her together, baby. Right here is where you belong." He placed my hand over his heart.

"What about my—"

"Sshhh... No more questions; let me show you."

THE NORMAL WORLD would say he ruined your life and stay away, but the way my body reacted to just the lightest touch of his hand brought me joy, protection, and comfort. Our lips tangled together, and we pulled at each other's clothes for relief and security. Seconds before he pulled my shirt off, a lightbulb went off in my head, and I pushed him away.

"Hold on, Sante."

"No, I need you," he growled, yanking me back to his chest.

I shook my head and pulled my shirt back down.

"Let's go home and have dinner. This is your parents' living room."

"I'm only hungry for one thing, taking you to my bedroom." When he picked me up, I automatically wrapped my legs around his waist, feeling his dick press against my stomach. I shouldn't be so engrossed in doing this in his parents' home. The look in his eyes conveyed no way he would let me go again, after everything that had happened. Carrying me up to his bedroom, a warm feeling surrounded me as he kissed me from my neck to my chest. When we reached the room, he shut the door with his foot, walked over to the bed, and gently placed me on it. He backed away and stared down at me with a watchful eye.

"I need your honesty, Rena."

"Okay."

"Can you forgive me truly and move forward in our marriage?"

Thinking back on the times I'd dealt with men, each and every one casted a shadow of only wanting me for my body and nothing else. When Sante came along, he challenged that and actively pushed me away. I knew at the stern way he talked to me at this office was a defense to avoid his true feelings.

"Real marriage, husband and wife. Plus supporting my work?"

"Yes, and I'll support your work," he grumbled, removing his shirt, then his pants.

At my smile, his thick, long shaft stood at attention, and he smirked.

"Even if I have to work around a lot of men, you'll control your temper?"

"Yes, baby. Can I have you now?" In response, he leaned down to kiss me, and I cupped both sides of his face, sucking his bottom lips.

"I forgive you and want to move forward in our marriage. This doesn't mean I want to be kept out of decisions that pertain to me." I held his chin up, and he nodded in agreement and ran a hand between us and cupped my sex.

"Everything about you I missed."

"You did?"

"Yes, I want us to always be like this, baby." He ripped my blouse, hurriedly unbuckled my pants, and tossed both to the floor. As he lowered my heels, I spread my legs out wearing only a thong. The dominance within Sante emerged, and he was intent on winning and bringing me to the brink.

"Sei l'unico/a per me."

"Prove it, husband." Sante hovered over me. I ran a hand up his back, and he moved to my left breast and squeezed it gently. I gasped and covered his hand with mine and watched him lower his head to dart out his tongue and suck on my stiff nipple.

"*Ti amore.*"

"Ahhh...!" Sante trailed kisses across my right breast, pinching my left nipple. My left leg spread wide, and he moved to lick over my pussy. His tongue slid in and sucked on my nub. I gripped the back of his head. My sex got wetter at his touch, and Sante circled over my clit and lapped up my juices. He then crawled back up and lined his member at my entrance and pushed forward. I grabbed his arms at the pain of him not being in me for so long; it felt like the first time we made love.

"Mother of God... Baby, I love you," he moaned. I opened my eyes to see our bodies connected.

"Sante!" I cried out. The sensation took hold, and I lifted my head to capture his lips.

"Fuck... this is us, baby," he growled, and the lust in his eyes shone down on me. I arched my back at the immense pressure and felt my body convulse. As our skin slapped together, he pulled out of me, dropped to the ground, and pushed my legs together. Flipping me on my stomach, he peppered kisses up my legs to my ass cheeks. He placed a bite on my left cheek and smacked my ass.

"Ohhhh... ahhh yes."

He guided his dick to my opening, thrusted forward, and pumped faster and faster. I heard him growl and grunt, speaking full Italian.

"Shit! No more separation, you're my wife."

"Yes... Okay."

"We understand each other. We are partners for life."

"I doooo..." I felt his seed release in me. Out of breath, he fell on my back and moved my hair sideways while kissing my cheeks. He pulled out of me, gripped the back of my head, and leaned in to suck on my lips. I stretched my leg over his waist, gripped his manhood, and glided down slowly.

"Sssss..." He gazed into my eyes lustfully.

"I'm yours, baby." He ran his hands along my thighs, up my stomach, and gripped my heavy jugs while I rocked back and forth.

"Ughhh... goddamn, you're leaking."

"About to come!"

Sante wrapped me around the waist, rotated me on my back, and pounded in me. His balls pushed against my ass when we came at the same time. Our bodies heaved up and down as we clasped hands and tightened our lips together.

"I'm taking you home."

"Let's go home."

TWENTY-SIX

SANTE

Two months later

"Please leave all messages with my assistant Nikki," Rena's voicemail explained, and I wanted to toss the phone out the window. I thought everything was fixed after we made love and promised to do right by each other. When I woke up this morning, Rena left a note and said she couldn't move forward. I tried to call Nikki and McKayla, and they both told me they weren't aware of her whereabouts, which I didn't believe.

"Sante."

I ignored my brother, slid my hands in my pocket, and looked out of the window of my office.

"She's not in New York."

"Where is she?"

"Not in the US."

I whipped around fast, glaring at him.

"Where is she, EJ?"

"I'm still working out the details. We have a few people that work for the TSA."

"Did they spot her?"

"They've narrowed it down to a few people."

He dumped a file on my desk.

"And?"

My chest tightened at the thought of her out in the world alone.

"The ten women we found had different-colored hair but based on Rena's features."

I sat at my desk, flipped through the file, and picked up a few photos of Rena in a blond wig, holding a shopping bag. One of them had her laughing at something a guy said.

"Who's the guy?"

"Nobody."

"Why is she laughing in his face!" I slammed the photo down on the desk.

"It's a bar, Sante."

"I want a flight out to this location."

"We don't know if she's still there."

"How long ago was this?"

"At least two days; she's smart."

"This is bullshit."

"You should have listened to me."

My brows hiked in suspension.

"You know where she is, don't you?"

"No."

"You're hiding her from me? Are you in on this with her?" I jumped out of my seat, and the door opened to reveal Renato.

"Did you tell him?" Vincenzo asked.

"He's irrational." EJ threw his hands up.

"Fuck you, EJ!"

"No, you've been an ass to all of us. We didn't fuck up

your marriage," EJ argued, pointing a finger at me, and I flipped him off.

"Get out."

"You can't control her, so you're taking it out on your family," EJ spat back, and I charged at him and threw a punch. He rubbed his jaw, tightened his fist, and pushed me forward.

"Sante, calm down!" Vincenzo shouted and tried to separate us. We fell over my desk with my back to the computer.

"I'm not on your payroll! Fuck you!" EJ yelled, punching me in the right side.

"Fuck!" I coughed, holding my side.

"That's enough!" Savio yelled, slamming the door behind him. EJ and I pulled away from each other.

"Get him out of here."

"Your problems are staring you in the mirror," Savio responded, marching over and standing in front of my face.

I looked from Vincenzo to EJ and back to Savio.

"Take it up for him."

"Stop acting like a child," Savio replied.

I growled, "I recall McKayla left you."

"I was fucked up about that and let her have a moment."

I waved them both off and walked around my desk to grab my keys, jacket, and photos.

"Where are you going?"

"To find my wife."

"She doesn't want to be found."

I stopped at the door and dropped my shoulders in defeat.

"Give her some time, Sante."

"I can't," I answered and left my office.

Knock! Knock!

"It's open."

As soon as I left my office, I drove over to a private detective we'd used in the past to gather information on enemies we wanted to eliminate. Dorsey wasn't the typical detective. He was retired from the Chicago PD for corruption. His skills were ruthless and dangerous, but he still could get information from local police friends we couldn't pay off.

"Sante. You haven't needed my services in months. This must be important." Dorsey reached out to shake my hand.

"I need your help."

"Sure, what's this about?"

"My wife."

"Your wife?"

"I got married a few months back."

"You of all people. Well, congrats."

"She left me."

He sipped on his coffee.

"Why?"

"I lied to her."

"How long has she been missing?"

"Two months."

"Shit, that's a long time."

"Can you help?"

"Maybe."

"What do you need?"

"Her last known location and numbers."

I handed him the photos EJ left with me and wrote her phone number down.

"She was supposed to be in New York, but we found that she was last seen out of the country."

"If I find her, do you want me to bring her back?"

"No, tell me but don't let her know you've found her."

"All right. I'll keep you updated."

"Thanks."

Buzz!

I peered down at my vibrating phone and saw some guys from the Colombo Family were getting into fights at the club, and the owner wanted me to kick them out since I was a partner.

"I need to go."

"Anything else I need to know?" Dorsey questioned.

"Keep your distance, but if she's with another man, kill him."

"That's extra."

"I'm good to pay."

I went to the car to head to *Bresi* strip club. It was still early at six in the afternoon. I had enough going on, and the Colombo Family acting like an ass interrupted me from trying to get Rena back. The limo arrived out front, and I told my driver to stay out here. I shut the door behind me, stomped inside, and saw the bartender standing with Paolo the manager and a few guys with harsh glares on their faces. I wanted to smash each face in with my fist.

"Paolo, what's going on?"

"Sante, thanks for coming."

"Gentlemen."

"They refuse to leave," Paolo said.

"We paid our money!" one of the guys barked, and my eyes twitched at the bass in his voice.

"Give them their money back."

"That's not how we work," the leader of the pack remarked.

"Do you know who I am?" I stepped closer to his face.

He grinned, tapping his men on the chest.

"Calabresi, right? You're the weak brother, right?"

That comment pissed me off, and I gripped him around the throat and bumped my forehead at his nose. Shoving him to the ground, I hammered my fist in his face.

"Sante!" Paolo yelled and tried to pull me off, and I jerked away.

"Argh!" the guy cried out.

"Show some fucking respect, you piece of shit!"

"Shoot him!" one of his other grimy friends shouted. I raised and removed my gun from my holster and pointed it at his face.

"Drop it! Get the fuck out of my club," I gritted through my teeth.

"Mmmm..." he moaned on the floor, and I kicked him in the stomach.

"Now!" I screamed, and they grabbed up their friend and carried him out of the club. Most of the staff stopped what they were doing to watch and waited as they left. My men came inside, and I didn't care if they would have shot me. All I kept thinking about was if Rena wasn't here, nothing else mattered.

"You all right?" Paolo asked, and I nodded.

"If you have more problems out of them, call Renato." I put the gun back in my holster and walked out to head home.

TWENTY-SEVEN

RENA

"Rena, what do you think of this design?" Abigail held up the piece of material she was using for a gown. I'd been in Paris for the past few weeks after leaving London. Before that, I was off to Aruba on the beach and took in the peace of being alone to get myself centered.

McKayla and Nikki both tried many times to get me to contact them, but I'd always tell them I would contact them when I was ready. All I did was shop, swim, eat, and drown in alcohol to get my thoughts of Sante out of my head. He'd become my everything so fast that I couldn't think without taking his opinion in the answers.

"It's beautiful."

"You should use it for your designs."

"What do you mean?"

"I've heard you crying in your sleep. You need to be more creative."

"You heard me?"

Abigail laid the gold material on the counter, locked

her arm in mine, and headed to her balcony, where we sat out with a glass of champagne.

"What did he do?"

"I can't say."

"It must have been bad if you are this distressed."

"My whole family is torn apart."

"He's in a business that calls for discretion, and you can't be allowed to talk to a friend. Only family."

"You know who my husband is?"

"Oh, don't worry, I have family in the business." She patted my hand.

"He killed my brother, and my mother hates me."

"In time, she'll come around."

"Not this time. We were so close. She blames me."

"Her feelings are valid."

I agreed. She picked up the champagne.

"Once you've taken the time to think over your feelings, it will be clear to you."

"Am I supposed to just be okay with everything he does?"

"No, you are supposed to speak your mind."

"I decided to go back."

"Marriage is not easy."

"I don't even think this marriage is going to last."

"Because?"

"My father left when I was younger, and I was raised by my mom. Sometimes I think Sante will turn out like him."

"You can't think like that. "

"You're right."

"Time to stop running."

"So, you're saying I need to go back home?"

"Can you tell yourself that you can live without him?"

"No, I can't," I sighed and pushed a piece of hair behind my ear.

"Then you need to go home and talk with your husband."

"Thank you, Abigail."

"You're welcome. I can have my private jet fly you home."

"You don't need to do that."

"Please, let me do something for you and Sante."

"Thank you."

An hour later, I was in the car as we pulled up to the airstrip, prepared to get out as she sat across from me. I gave her another hug and watched the driver take my luggage out and load it on the plane. I saw Abigail talk with the stewardess and pilot.

"Call me when you make it home safe," Abigail requested, and I rubbed the top of her shoulder.

"Welcome aboard, Mrs. Calabresi," the stewardess introduced herself.

"Thank you."

A week later

I dropped my bag at the door, removed my shades, and took in the condo I left two months ago, reminding myself why I went in the first place. Everything looked like it was still in place, except more light broke through the windows. The guards were surprised when they saw me walk up, and I couldn't do anything but apologize for disappearing without a trace. I felt like I was on the run with the way I hid out in different hotels and used other names. It was worth the sanity I had left to gather my thoughts and know if this was the life I wanted. I headed to the kitchen, opened the fridge, and saw it was full of food. I checked the cabinet and went to pull a bottle of wine from the rack and popped it open to pour a glass.

Ring!

"Hello."

I answered the call before McKayla sent out a search party.

"Finally, you answered."

"Sorry, I told you when I would be back."

"Doesn't make me feel better that you left without telling me."

"I needed to get away."

"Understandable, Rena, but we're family."

"You're right."

"Have you seen him?"

"Not yet."

"From what I heard, he's a lot colder to people."

"I can't imagine he'll be ready to talk with open arms."

"Maybe I need to be there?"

"No, McKayla. I can't run to you for every problem."

"You're not. I've been in your place."

"That's true, but it's different."

"Have you spoken to Nikki?"

"Not yet. You were my first call."

"What about your mother?"

"That's another story."

"Remember where you've come from in this. Know your rights in how you feel."

"I cut him off completely and forced you and Nikki not to call me."

"Savio told me that Sante hired a PI."

"What?"

"Yeah."

"That's insane."

"We married them, but you shouldn't have slept with him again."

"That was my regret afterward because I gave false hope."

"You did."

"Maybe we need counseling."

"No, you did the right thing."

"Are you sure?"

"You can't second guess yourself."

Slam!

My head lifted at the sound of the door closing, and I glanced up at the dark pair of eyes with a scowl on his face.

"McKayla, let me call you back."

"Is that him?"

"Yes."

"Do you need me to come over?"

"I'll be fine."

I ended the call, eased it down, and placed it in my pocket.

"I wasn't expecting you so late." I moved back toward the counter. He stalked over and closed the space between us.

"Where have you been?"

"Away."

"Clearly!"

"Sante, don't yell at me."

His chest rose and fell.

"You left without telling anyone. Do you know how this could have ended?"

"Are we going to talk?"

"Where did you go?"

"I flew to Paris."

He softened at my response.

"Baby."

"No, listen, I need time because I don't want to be stupid over you."

"You said you would forgive me."

"And I will, but you can't tell me when."

He brushed a hand down his face.

"You're right."

"Paris helped me to remember our connection, and I do need to let Ted go."

"You scared me."

"I heard you hired a private detective."

"He's supposed to be the best, but you left the last place too fast."

"London was beautiful."

"I don't care what we go through, Rena, running is not an option."

"I agree."

"Did you find what you were looking for?"

Sante pulled me into his chest, and I extended my arms around his neck.

"I realized that Ted would never stop, and I had to learn it the hard way."

Sante lifted my chin with his hand.

"My family is your family."

TWENTY-EIGHT

RENA

The next day

There was something about waking in my own home and bed that reminded me of what I missed out on while I was away. I looked to my right and saw the side of the bed that Sante slept on and wondered where he was. We came straight home and had sex two more times and didn't fall asleep until after midnight. I pushed the covers back, stood, and walked to the bathroom. In the shower, I let the water run over my back and chuckled at the hickeys on my inner thighs and wrists. Using the wash cloth and body soap, I closed my eyes and washed my chest, trying to visualize Sante's lips on every single part of my body. Ten minutes later, I stepped out, dried off, and stood in front of the mirror.

"Terrible," I muttered to myself.

"Cara!"

"Yes!"

"Breakfast is ready."

"Coming."

The smell wafted through the house, and my stomach

growled, which reminded me I hadn't eaten since before yesterday afternoon.

"You cooked breakfast." I brushed my shoes on the floor by the table, walked up to Sante's back, and wrapped my arms around his waist.

"How did you sleep?"

"Amazing."

"I apologize again."

"You've apologized enough, Sante. I won't hold this against you."

He dropped the spatula and whipped around in my arms, putting his hands on my waist and leaning against the counter.

"What are your plans today?"

"Shopping and lunch with Nikki and McKayla."

"Do you want me to come with you?"

"No, it will be fine."

"My men will be there."

"What are you doing today?"

"I have a meeting to go over the trucking business."

"Is everything all right?"

"Yeah, my family wants to have dinner."

"Do you mind if I bring Mom?"

"Do you think that would work?"

I extended around him, picked up a sausage from the pan, and broke off a piece in my mouth.

"Honestly, I have no clue. She hasn't taken any of my calls. I'm content with what he did and that he knows he had enemies."

"I want her to be comfortable."

"You're right, I'll give her time, before I call her again."

"What about your fashions?"

"I met with Nikki and will get the ball rolling again."

He grabbed the pancakes and put them in the middle of the table. I rubbed my stomach and scanned the sausages, fruit, biscuits, cinnamon rolls, and scrambled eggs.

"I'm starving."

"Dinner won't be too late."

"Is Marilyn cooking?"

"Probably, along with my mother and Cora."

"How is she doing?"

"Good. I think she likes EJ."

I choked on my orange juice.

"Are they dating?"

"I don't think so."

"So why do you think she likes him?"

He wiped his mouth of the syrup and fruit juices. I cut into the pancake and eggs and tossed them into my mouth.

"Just a feeling I have but tell me about your business."

"I have to call Nikki to set up the vendors again, because I canceled it at first.

"Do you need money?"

"I don't want you to pay for everything. McKayla wants to invest."

"My money is your money, cara."

"The show is in New York," I blurted out, drinking my coffee.

"When?"

"In a few weeks, maybe a month."

"Can that be pulled off?"

"We had things already started. It's just a matter of putting things in place."

"Then I'll do whatever I can do to help."

"Thank you."

"Anything for you." He moved around the table, lifted my chin, and kissed me on the lips.

HOURS LATER, I stepped out of the car as the bodyguards guided me to the front entrance, where I met up with Nikki and McKayla standing at the front of Nordstrom.

"As usual, you're late." McKayla rolled her eyes, and I flipped her off.

"Sorry, I was a little caught up."

"Caught up with whom?" Nikki teased, picking up a pair of shoes from the rack.

"Sante and I made up."

"As in staying married?" McKayla probed. I walked around to check the sale on the boots.

"Yes. I went to talk to him at his parents' house."

"I'm happy for you," McKayla said.

"He listened to me because I was ready to leave officially." I placed the shoes back down on the stand.

"I remember the mess with Savio."

"You two sound like you've been through some rough times," Nikki implied.

"He's onboard with the business and New York."

"You're putting the fashion show back on?" Nikki tested the waters.

"Yep, and I need you to contact all the vendors."

"I can do that. It might cost a little extra."

"Money is no object."

"Did you tell him I was investing?" McKayla asked.

"I did. He wanted to put money in the business, but I want this to be my own."

We headed to the dress section, and I picked up a red cocktail dress.

"What do you think about this for dinner tonight?" I posed.

"Cute, shows your shape," Nikki answered.

"How is my godson?" I held the dress on my arm and picked up a black pants suit.

"Spoiled by his father and uncles. I barely got a moment with him," McKayla complained, and I chuckled.

"Fathers and their boys."

"What did he say about your brother?" McKayla probed.

"You know we've talked growing up. We were close until maybe around high school."

"All I can say is that you need to keep communication open."

"This is why I'll continue dating and skip marriage," Nikki joked.

I headed to the store clerk to pay for the dress. My cell vibrated, and I pulled it out to see a text from Sante about my fashion event.

Sante: Amore, when is your trip to New York?

Me: We decided two months from now.

Sante: I'll get us a condo in the city.

Me: You don't have to do that, babe. I can stay with Nikki.

Sante: I plan on doing a lot of things with you and need privacy.

I giggled at his response and looked up at McKayla's teasing expression.

"I know that look," Nikki implied.

"What look?"

"The look of love. I ended up with a baby."

"No babies over here. I like it just being me and Sante."

"Does Sante know that?"

"Yes, we've talked about it, and he knows."

"Good, what is he texting about?"

Me: Okay... baby.

I put my cell back in my pocket and grabbed the receipt from the counter, thanking her.

"Let's go. He just said he's getting us a condo in New York."

"No more girl nights."

"Nope. I guess I turned into McKayla, an old married wife now."

"Hey, my marriage isn't old." McKayla frowned and drew her face into a snarl.

~

Conversation flowed as we sat around the table and laughed about Savio getting peed on, while McKayla was out shopping and having a girls day.

"That's not funny, Renato," Savio scoffed, punching in his arm.

"Fuck, man," Renato snarled, looking him up and down.

"Savio, do you want more kids?" I grilled and picked up my glass of water.

I wore the red cocktail dress, left my hair down bone straight.

"Rena, tell me about your fashion show?" Adelina asked, pouring more wine in her glass.

"It's going to be my debut look that sets up my brand."

"In New York, correct?"

"Yes, ma'am. I'm excited."

"I'm glad you and Sante were able to work out your issues."

He placed his hand on my thigh under the table, and I laid my palm on top and squeezed.

"We've secured a place in New York to stay without having to deal with hotels," Sante mentioned, and my heart buzzed in anticipation of having my dreams come true.

"Rena, are you two going to have a honeymoon?" Adelina pressed.

I looked at Sante, and he smiled.

"We didn't have the most conventional wedding, I guess we can take a trip."

"If she wants to take a honeymoon," Sante spoke, extending his hand to cup my chin.

"Maybe, but it'll have to wait until the show is over."

"Love that my boys have found women who bring out the best in them," Adelina toasted. McKayla leaned her head on Savio, and I pecked Sante on the cheek.

"You still have three more to marry off," I teased, and Renato scoffed. I cackled at his annoyed expression.

"No marriage for me, just like my brother Renato," Vincenzo spouted.

"Wait until the right woman comes along." Mr. Calabresi winked his left eye at his sons.

Marilyn came into the dining room and placed slices of cake on the table. I rubbed my stomach, feeling full.

"I'm stuffed. I can't have anything else."

"Marilyn makes the best lemon cake," Adelina said, picking up the fork and biting into her slice.

"Thank you, Adelina," Marilyn replied and took our leftover dishes to the kitchen.

I wiped my mouth and tossed my napkin on the table, laughing at Savio poking at McKayla.

Ding!

Everyone looked up at the doorbell ringing and Renato pulled out his gun.

"Put that away, Renato," Adelina fussed as the house manager walked in with a surprising guest.

"Mom." I walked around the table and pulled her by the hand to the hallway.

"I tried calling you, but didn't get an answer," she replied, glancing back at the dining room.

"What's wrong?"

"I needed to talk about moving."

"What?"

"You've made a life for yourself, and I'm proud of you, but I can't stay here."

"Where are you moving?"

"To Ohio, somewhere quiet and peaceful."

"You can't just make a decision like this."

"Honey, you don't need me."

"I always need you."

"Rena, what's going on?" Sante walked up on us, and my mom glared at him.

"I'd appreciate privacy while I talk to my daughter," she snapped.

"Mom."

"Mrs. Clark, I know you may have hated me."

"Hate is too good for you. You killed my child!" she yelled, and my heart dropped.

"Can we talk about this later?" I tried to lead her out of the house.

"No, I already made plans to sell the house."

"But what about me?"

"Rena, you can always come visit, but your life is here now with these people," she explained, and I fidgeted with my hands.

"You're serious about this?

"Yes, I'll send you my address once I settle everything."

She hugged me tight, and I held her close as tears pooled in my eyes.

"Do you need anything? Any money?"

"No, I have the money from the sale of the house," she said. I didn't want to let her go. At the same time, I couldn't force her to change her decision.

"I'm sorry about your son."

Slap!

When she lifted her palm over his face, I gasped.

"Mom!" She shook her head and ran toward the door. I followed to stop her, but Sante pulled me back into the house.

"I'm sorry."

He rubbed my back up and down.

"She has the right to be upset."

"I've never seen her act this way." We watched her drive off the property.

"Are you okay, Rena?" McKayla approached me, and I collapsed in her arms.

"What was that about?" Adelina probed, and I shook my head.

"Her mother was just here. She's upset," Sante announced, pulling me into his chest as I wiped my eyes.

"What can I do, honey?" she asked.

"Nothing, I'll be fine. It's going to take time."

"Do you want to go home?" Sante asked.

"Yeah, I might need that honeymoon right now." I pouted, laying my head back on his chest.

"Then your wish is my command." He moved a piece of my hair behind my ear and kissed my forehead.

"Thank you, Adelina. Sorry to mess up your dinner."

"Never apologize, Rena. We're family and when one hurts, we all hurt." Adelina extended a hand to my shoulder.

"Let's get going," Sante announced, walking over to the closet to grab my coat and purse.

"Call me when you're up to talk."

"I will."

TWENTY-NINE

SANTE

Two days later

"So, this meeting was initiated by you, Sante?" Alize sat back in his chair. His entire face was balled into anger, and I watched each man mimic his expression as my brother forced him to go along with our plans.

"With my awareness," Savio answered and sat back as I stood in front of all the bosses.

"It failed previously, how do we know it won't happen again."

"Alize, you know I can understand your hesitation, but this is a deal that we can't miss."

"How do we fair in this deal?"

"Serbians won't work with anyone but me."

"That's because you went behind our backs!" Tommaso shouted. My fist clenched, wanting to punch him in the face.

"You'll get your cut, Tommaso. Don't worry."

"Little prick," he mumbled, and Alize extended a hand over to stop him from getting up. If he wanted a fight, I was ready, but I'd hate to bury another leader of a family so soon after the senator.

"Serbians are getting guns and drugs run through the trucks, but we're only getting a small piece," Alize reminded me, and I knew he would bring that up.

"We have the most risk."

"Because you went and fucked us over," Terzo, one of Colombo's underlings muttered. Renato grasped him around the collar.

"Say one more thing, and I'll cut your tongue out." Renato threatened, and I grinned.

"Renato," Savio called his name.

"Your father would never do business like this," Alize remarked. He just didn't know that my father was onboard with us shaking things up.

"Our way of business still gives you money."

"But no voting power," Tommaso commented.

"Carmine fucked that up when he tried to kill my wife."

"Something you put in motion early on," Terzo barked. I was ready to end his life right now.

"On the advice of our leader and consulting with our lawyer, we want all of Colombo's territory reversed over to us."

Terzo jumped up to charge at me.

"Grab him!" a guard shouted, and I stood in place.

"What are you doing, Savio?" Alize scolded.

"Sante is running things."

"We're getting Colombo, and you'll both get two percent of the funds from the Serbians, but we own all voting rights," I explained.

Alize put his cigar out in the ashtray.

"Tommaso, say something."

"Shut up!" Alize yelled back.

"He has all the cards," Tommaso expressed.

"I hope you know what you're doing, Sante." Alize sighed and sat back in his seat.

Tommaso looked around the room at my brothers, then back at me.

"If we decline?" Tommaso challenged, and I looked at Savio, leaning forward with his hands clasped together.

"We want to be in business together, gentlemen."

"You have my vote." Alize rose from his seat, and my guards waited to see what his next move would be, but he headed to the door.

"That was your last friend in this business, kid," Tommaso expressed.

"Do we have your vote?"

"With my arms tied, you have my vote," Tommaso snarled, and the other hands raised. Terzo shook his head, stood, and removed his gun, which caused my guards to remove theirs.

Pop! Pop!

~

"What are you doing here?"

I placed the stack of papers on my father's desk and removed my jacket.

"I wanted to stop in before I head back to New York."

"How did the meeting go?"

"Terzo is dead."

He stared at me with a watchful eye, rubbing his chin.

"Did he make a move first?"

"He didn't like our decision."

"That was going to be the outcome no matter what."

"Do you think I was wrong?"

"If your motivation was in the right place, then no."

"He would have come after us to avenge Carmine's death."

"I sensed that the moment word got back to Alize."

"Brambilla thinks I'm over my head."

"We've all been young and dumb in this business."

"As long as I have your approval, I'll sleep easy at night."

"What do you have to do tomorrow?"

"Meeting with Serbians."

"Are you flying back for Rena's event?"

"Hopefully, if we wrap up everything."

"Be careful with them."

"Renato and Savio are coming with me."

"ACE was a brilliant idea."

"Thanks, Papa."

"You and Savio have become a combination of your grandfather."

I smirked. "How so?"

"Ruthless."

"Learned from the bet."

"Go see your mother; she's missing you."

I extended my hand to shake his and left the documents for him to look over. Walking out of his office, I headed to the kitchen to talk with my mother. Cora and Marilyn were sitting with her. I kissed each one on the forehead and gave them a hug.

"How long are you in town for?" Cora asked.

"Not long. I have to try to get back in time for Rena's show."

"I wish I was going," Cora whined. I pulled on her ear like I used to do when she was a little kid.

"If you're the boss, why can't you get help to cover you?"

"Doesn't work like that, Sante. I don't have billions of dollars in my account." She punched me in the arm.

"I told you we'd give you money for anything."

"I don't want your money."

"Leave her alone, Sante. Cora has worked hard without us, and she doesn't want a handout," Mother explained. I understood; Rena was the same way. All the women in my life didn't take handouts from the men. We had to practically sneak it into their hands.

"Have you talked to Rena's mother?" Marilyn probed and moved the basket of potatoes into the sink.

"Rena told me to give her time."

"Here, try this?" Mom pushed a spoon of red sauce toward me. Testing the flavors, I nodded it was perfect.

"That was her real brother?" Cora asked.

"Yeah." I sighed and sat next to her at the counter.

"Can you get me a discount on her clothes?"

"Where's Elio?"

"I don't know."

"He wasn't at the meeting."

"Well, maybe he had a date," Cora answered as she closed the book she was reading and slid out of the chair.

"You seem angry."

"Sante," Mom scolded me.

"What?" I shrugged my shoulders.

"It's okay, Adelina. Sante's always been an ass," Cora muttered and stuck her tongue out at me.

"I'll try again with her. I know it's important to Rena that we get along."

"For the family's sake, what was your meeting about

today?" Mom demanded and wiped her hands on the dish towel.

"Expanding business." I kept it vague. She knew enough but not everything that we were doing after my father retired.

"Nothing that would have the police at our door, right?" She hiked a brow at me.

"No, Madre, all good," I responded, helping her move the steaks into the oven.

"All right, are you staying for dinner?"

Lifting my hand, I checked my watch for the time.

"No, I have something I need to do." I kissed her on the cheek, then Marilyn, and left the house.

"Where to, boss?" Roddy, my new driver asked.

"To the airstrip."

"Going to New York?"

"Not yet."

He drove off my parents property, and I contemplated what I would say to Rena's mother try to make amends. She had every right to hate me, but she still had one child. It wasn't right to push Rena away because of a decision I made, even if I had my reasons. Two hours later, I arrived on the doorstep of her mother's home. It was a smaller one-story family home in the suburbs. It looked like most residents were home in bed as lights on the street were on. I knocked on the door and waited with bated breath, a nervousness I usually didn't have unless it was Rena.

"Sante." She looked confused. I must have disturbed her sleep because she was wearing a robe and scarf on her head.

"Can I come inside?" I asked.

She pushed the door open and stepped to the side to allow me to enter.

"What are you doing here?"

I peered around the small living room that held photos of Rena and Ted as kids on the walls.

"I'm sorry it's late. I wanted to talk to you."

"Is Rena all right?"

"She's fine."

"Okay, sit."

"We didn't get off on the right foot."

"I guess we didn't."

"Rena means a lot to me."

"She means a lot to me as well."

"Rena told you she left me when all this happened with Ted?"

"Yes."

"I was miserable for days."

"I would think so."

"Rena loves you, and you're all she has."

"I'll speak to my daughter when I'm ready."

"Don't shut her out because of me."

"As I told her, it's going to take time. I know Ted did some terrible things, but he was my son."

"My mother would say the same thing about me."

"Does she know you're here?"

"No one knows."

"Rena briefly told me her brother stole money."

"Among other things, he owed a mutual associate money, but the ultimate offense was trying to get Rena killed."

"Are you positive about that?"

I pulled out my phone and went to the video saved on my phone and pressed play.

"What's this?"

"Just watch."

I was saving this as backup if I ever needed evidence, no matter if the police or a rival family came at me. Ted was going to be taken out for his disloyalty, and the video showed him on camera with Carmine as he gave him the green light to hurt his sister.

Darla gasped in shock, and tears slipped from her eyes as a hand gripped her lips.

"He really tried to hurt my baby," she mumbled, passing the phone back to me. I passed her a hand-kerchief.

"Sorry, I had to show you that video. I had no choice."

"In the beginning, he was determined to make a change in public life."

"Maybe that's true, but along the way, he gambled too much."

"Probably how he afforded my last home."

"Do you think you could make up with Rena?"

"I will. Thank you."

"That's all I hope for."

"Her show is coming up, right?"

"In a week."

"I'll have to try to get there."

I reached in my pocket, pulled out a business card, and wrote down the number to my pilot.

"Call this number when you're ready."

"Who is this?"

"My personal pilot. We can have the plane here in no time."

"Rena is really important to you."

"My life."

"Glad to hear that."

"Thank you for listening to me, Darla."

"I didn't expect you to come all the way out here, but that shows you're committed to my daughter."

"She's given me something I can't take back."

"What?"

"Love."

After another hug, I stood and walked to the door as Darla held it open.

"Don't forget to call that number."

Back in the car, I removed my phone and looked at my messages.

Me: Baby, I love you.

Rena: Who is this?

Me: Who do you think it is?

Rena: Husband, is that you?"

Me: The only husband you'll ever have.

Rena: Till death do us part.

Me: Even in the afterlife, I'll find you.

THIRTY

RENA

A month later

"Where do you want this?" I heard someone calling out to me as I directed the movers on where to put the couch in our condo in New York. After that night at Sante's parents' home, we came here to have a little break from the family. I also needed to get things prepared for my show. McKayla flew out yesterday to help me, while Sante and Savio handled business. Sante stuck to his promise of supporting me, and I couldn't ask for a better husband.

"You can hang it near the window," I explained to Nikki as she held two paintings that Sante had shipped here.

"Have you spoken to your mom?" McKayla sat on the floor, unwrapping some dishes and placing them on the table.

"I talked to her a week ago. She's going to be at the show." I smiled, thinking about getting to bond again with my mom. Once she moved down, I flew to Ohio and stayed with her for a few days. We talked about the things that Ted did and how it would have caused me to get hurt. Finally, she understood the decisions that Sante made and forgave him. Even my mother-in-law came with me one time to visit, and the family got closer to her and included her in any family functions.

"So happy you two have reconnected," McKayla replied.

"We have to walk through the venue in two hours," Nikki said, picking up a box of dishes and moving them to the kitchen.

"I'll be ready."

"Did you get any media to come?" McKayla asked as she picked up the dishes and headed to the kitchen.

"Nikki was able to get a PR company to contact some media outlets. It was more about them coming for Rena Fashions and not Rena Calabresi."

The moving guys brought in the desk and chairs for my office as I sauntered to my bedroom to grab an outfit for later tonight.

"Guess who?" He wrapped his arm around my waist and covered my eyes with his right hand.

"Payton, you better hurry up before my husband finds you,"

He bit the side of my neck, and I giggled.

"Who the fuck is Payton? He pushed me up against the drawer and pulled my head to plant a kiss on my cheek.

"I don't know."

"You like playing with me, don't you?"

I grinned and felt his hands move across my ass.

"He's nothing, and you know that... ugh!" I felt a slap to my ass.

"If you find out who he is, you better tell him to pray."

"Are you jealous?"

"Are you mine, or do I need to remind you?"

"Maybe you can remind me, but I have to get dressed."

"Where are you going?" I slipped out of his hold, walked to the closet that had been redone to my liking. It was two floors, and Sante had his own closet down the hall. Our entire penthouse was worth over twenty million dollars.

"The venue. Nikki and I need to do a run through."

"How long will that be?"

"Maybe an hour or two." He followed me in the closet. I looked through the clear cabinets that housed shirts. Everything was color coordinated by specific item.

"Will we have any alone time before the show?"

"I'm sorry. Once everything is finalized, I'll make it up to you."

"I have to fly back to Chicago."

"What? I thought you'd be here the whole time."

He shook his head.

"Some business I need to take care of with my brothers."

"Business."

"Yes, and if I didn't have to handle this, you know I would be at your show."

"Okay, Sante."

"Are you disappointed?"

"No, I knew what this life would bring."

"Promise to make it up to you soon."

"When do you leave?"

"Tonight."

"Be safe. Is McKayla flying back with you?"

"Yeah, but she might come back up here."

"So, it's just me and Nikki."

"Not forever, cara."

He pressed a kiss to my lips.

Nikki talked to the venue coordinator, and I got the keys early to do the walkthrough after I kissed Sante goodbye a few hours ago. We came straight to the location, and it was massive. The pictures online didn't do it any justice. New York had a vibe that came with high fashion but grit at the same time. My designs could be worn by anyone, and I wanted to make a statement to the world that Rena made it here not by my husband's money but hard work.

"I want the colors to be sleek, maybe off white Egyptian."

"That would be pretty." Nikki took notes.

"We want the brand to stand the test of time."

"Are you going with a live DJ?"

"What do you think?"

"It could work, but you don't want to distract from the models."

"That's true."

"Keep it as an option, but I'm not stuck on that."

The back area would house the makeup, bathrooms, and food area. I had over two thousand square feet of space to play around and set to my liking.

"I want the media to be in their own sections." I pointed to the right corner of the room just below the stage.

"Are the models doing a walk tonight?" I wondered. We were a week away from show time.

"Should be arriving shortly."

"Great, I can't believe this is happening."

"Believe it because you're going to be a star."

"Thanks, Nikki. You're the one who knew I had a gift and supported me before anyone else."

"Happy to see you doing something you love."

"With your help."

"Come on, we need to eat."

"Do you want to order in or go out?"

"A restaurant is around the corner. We have an hour before the girls show up."

"That's fine."

"I forgot your bodyguards need to know the change of plans," she joked as we marched out the door. They stood at attention and opened the car door when photographers popped out of nowhere.

"Mrs. Calabresi! Are you ready for the show?"

"No comment."

"Will your husband be there?"

I walked around him, and he blocked me off. The guard started to shove him away.

"It's fine," I expressed, standing for a few shots. It was funny how I became the story instead of being the person that wrote the story.

"What can you tell us about your husband's business?"

"He's a businessman like anyone else."

"He's backing your fashion event, correct?"

"No, I have my own money." I lied but didn't want to go into detail of the million dollars that came from me marrying Sante.

"No more questions." Nikki blocked his camera. I slid in the car, and she climbed in behind me.

"Ugh, I hate this."

"They'll find another story to talk about."

The car pulled into traffic, and Nikki told them to go toward the sandwich shop.

Ring!

I grabbed my phone from my pocket and answered.

"Hey."

"I needed to hear your voice."

"You called right on time."

"Everything okay?"

"Just some photographers being nosy."

"Did they touch you?"

"No, stop worrying."

"My job is to worry."

The limo stopped, and Donato our driver stepped out and came to my side and opened the door.

"Nothing for you to worry about."

"Did the walk through go well?"

"It did, and we're stepping out for lunch now."

"Call me after you get home so I can put you to bed."

"Are you being naughty, Mr. Calabresi?"

"For you, I can be naughty or nice."

Nikki spoke with the hostess, and I trailed behind to the table near the back corner.

"We just got a table. I'll call you later."

"Don't forget to call me when you make it home."

"Yes, Mr. Calabresi."

He groaned, and I laughed at his annoyance with me. I would never be something I wasn't, and that kept him guessing as my husband. He thought as a single woman, I drove him crazy. It would only get worse now that we were in the marriage for real.

"Thank you." I took the menu from the hostess and placed my phone on the table before removing my coat.

"What are you thinking of getting?"

"Probably the usual. We only have an hour before the girls will arrive."

"We can always get it to go."

"I'll take the usual tuna and fries."

"Did you remember to get gift bags for the guests?" I rambled off questions, closing my menu as the waitress arrived at our table.

"I did."

"Hello, are you getting the usual, Rena?" Susan, our usual server, asked.

"Susan, you know my show is coming up, right?"

"I heard about the fashion show."

"I need the works on my sandwich and a large shake."

"Coming up right away. Are you excited?" Susan asked, and I smiled.

"Excited can't describe how ready I am to get this going."

"You've been all over the news, a local celebrity."

"That's the funny part, because I feel like little Rena from Chicago."

"It'll change." Susan laughed and took our menus.

"She's right. Look at how far you've come over the past few months," Nikki said.

"I guess if Sante were here, I'd feel a little more confident."

"Maybe try to ask him to come again."

"He has too much work back home."

"Married life is different."

"I used to say that about McKayla and told myself I'd never get married."

"We grow and change."

"Grow and change."

Susan came to the table with our drinks, and I picked up the straw to sip on the strawberry milkshake.

THE TUB FILLED with hot water, and I stepped my feet in to test it out before sliding down slowly and letting the hot steam soothe my bones. Nikki and I didn't leave the venue after lunch until around midnight, and I came straight to the condo and poured a glass of wine, lit some candles, and let myself relax to get the stress out of my system. Everything was in place, and I couldn't back out now if I wanted because all the payments were finalized. Nikki went back to her place and would meet with me again to discuss any last-minute details, but I told her to take the next day off. We'd exhausted our nerves by checking and rechecking every detail to the last minute, and there wasn't anything else to change.

"Mhmmmm..."

Ring!

I popped my eyes open and reached for the phone to see Sante FaceTime me. I answered, placing the wine glass on the tray in front of me.

"You forgot to call me."

"Hey, handsome."

"What are you doing?"

"Taking a bath."

"You look tired."

"Exhausted."

"You get everything finished?"

I yawned and covered my mouth.

"Yeah, we're all set."

"Did the movers finish everything?"

"We just need to open a few more boxes."

"When I get back in town, I'll handle that."

"I can hire someone, babe, or do it myself later."

"I don't want my wife to overwork herself."

The right corner of my lip curved upwards.

"Your wife."

"Love saying those words."

"Sante."

"Yeah, baby."

I stared at his face as he lay in bed with no shirt on.

"Nothing."

"Why the long face?" he pressed.

"Just missing you is all."

"We'll be together soon."

"Not soon enough."

"Work can't be helped."

"I know, but anyway, tell me about your day."

"We signed more truckers and expanded into Canada."

"Soon you'll be a double billionaire," I joked, and he smiled, running his tongue across his lips.

"You'll be a double billionaire, anything I have is yours."

"I like the sound of that."

"Get your ass to bed."

"Or what are you going to do, spank me?"

A look of arousal crossed his face.

"Just for that, when I see you, I'll do more than a spanking."

"Tell me."

"My tongue will run up the crest of your neck, to your full lips, and down to that sweet, tight sex."

"You're getting me all wet."

"Good that I'm not there then. I'd have you up all night long."

"A good spanking never hurt anyone."

"Rena..." he groaned.

"Yes. husband." I giggled, hung up the phone, and picked up the wine glass, thinking about all the dirty things Sante would do to me.

CHAPTER

THIRTY-ONE

SANTE

he next day

The guys finally locked in the contract to expand ACE Trucking into new territory and gave us extra time to wash any dirty money. The Serbians passed the five million dollars over in small bills, and we agreed on two trucks to carry their crates of guns monthly. I stood off to the side with my brothers Savio and Renato as we loaded everything up. Savio took a little bit of a break from the business to help with the baby, and I led most of the meetings to get them back to the table even though I'd brought a little attention from the media with Ted's killing. He nodded at me and I proceeded with the announcement.

"Gentlemen, it's done." I slapped Renato on the back.

"What's the word?" Renato asked.

"We take over Colombo's turf officially."

He masked his excitement, while the team shook hands with each other. The other families hesitated with us doing this underhanded, but I didn't care to explain myself after I closed the biggest deal we'd ever seen.

Either they'd get on board, or we'd have to find a way to achieve our goals in another way. Rena sent photos almost every day leading up to the show, and I'd planned on skipping out of this meeting, but I didn't trust anyone around my family.

"Sante, I take it we won't have any more problems?" Vlado wondered, and I reached a hand out to shake.

"No more problems on my end, Vlado. Renato will send you the address of the next drop off."

"Renato, Savio. Nice seeing you again." Vlado headed to his car. Our drivers loaded out behind his car to follow.

"What's next?" Renato asked.

"A few calls have come in from Mexico."

"You want to fly down to Mexico?" Savio asked.

"Not now, but I think it's something to think about."

"Investigate first and see what it looks like," Savio encouraged me, and I understood his worry as the oldest. I learned from this experience that making quick decisions could cost me more than my life.

"For now, I'm going to see my wife."

"Are any of the models cute?" Renato questioned, and I popped him on the back of the head.

"That's all you think about."

"What? Pussy?"

"Yeah." I opened the back door of the car.

"It's been awhile. That last one was a stripper at the club you frequent."

"Gentleman's club, and they don't call them strippers," I argued.

"That's what you think." Renato grinned.

Renato would never change. We'd given up on trying to get him to settle down and find someone. All he focused on was money, guns, and family.

"We need to go. My plane is standing by for me."

～

RENA STOOD off to the side of the announcer, and I made sure our guards had the entire room protected. She was the most precious thing in this room. I'd told her I couldn't make it to her show today, but McKayla came to support her, along with my mother and Rena's mom. The look in Rena's eyes as her mother sat in awe was the biggest reason I wanted her to share this moment with her daughter.

"Ladies and gentlemen, Designs by Rena has been picked up by over thirty national and international stores around the world!" her assistant announced over the microphone, to loud cheers and applause engulfing the room. My chest swelled with pride at how much she'd become a boss in her own right. I was ready to take her back home and celebrate one on one, but I knew she'd need to make her rounds of interviews and party stops for the next few days in New York. Even though we had our place here, Chicago was our main base. She'd been reorganizing this ever since we moved here, plus handling the show. I even talked her into doing some of her business online to bring in another revenue stream and look into brick-and-mortar stores. I signed off on a loan for her, even though I could have given her the money. She didn't want to take anything from me.

"Thank you for all of the support. I truly appreciate you and my team for putting this together," Rena remarked, standing on the stage. "This dream wouldn't be possible without my best friends McKayla, Nikki, and someone I call my biggest protector and fiercest opponent, Sante Calabresi." She laughed, and the crowd joined in on her joke. "So many times, we wanted to kill each other, but we stuck it out. Now, we're more in love than ever before."

I stepped on the stage, and the crowd went wild, cheering as I carried the twelve dozen roses. I didn't make it a habit to show my face in public, but to show my support, I came here to give her these flowers and make up for us being apart for the last few days. She lifted her hand over her face, with tears in her eyes. I grabbed her around the waist and captured her lips, still holding the roses in my left hand. She wrapped her arm around my neck, I dipped her back as our tongues fought for control. Flashes of light brought me out of my dark thoughts of fucking her in front of everyone. She pulled back from me and wiped the residue of her lipstick from my lips.

"What are you doing here?"

"I wanted to surprise you."

"Oh my God! Sante, these are beautiful."

"*Woohoo!*" the crowd cheered.

"Beauty that matches you."

"I can't believe you're here."

"Anything for you, Rena."

"Did you guys know he was coming?" Rena pointed at McKayla and Nikki. McKayla nodded and blew a kiss at Rena.

"Again, I want to thank everyone for coming today, especially you, Sante."

I winked at her.

"Please enjoy the rest of the show. Good night everyone!" Rena shouted and bowed. Leaning into my shoulder, we walked off to a standing ovation. My men secured a path for us to step off the stage and head to her dressing room. Nudging us inside, I shut the door and gently pushed her up against the back of the door. I pressed my hard on against her stomach, grasped both sides of her hips, sucked on her neck.

"Mmmmm..." she moaned.

"I want you now," I grunted, kneading her ass.

"We can go back to my hotel room."

I parted my lips and pulled back.

"I'm proud of you."

"Thank you." As she removed my tie, I leaned down to bite her cheek gently.

Knock! Knock!

"Go away!" she shouted.

I chuckled and pulled back.

"Rena, you have some reporters that want to interview you," Nikki replied.

She groaned and stopped midway from unzipping my pants.

"I will do this as quickly as I can."

"I'll wait. Don't be too long." I gripped my stiff dick in her hand, as she squeezed him, and I growled.

"Be good."

"Never." She kissed me again, stepped out of my hold, and left to do a few interviews as I redressed.

THE NEXT DAY

"Oohhh, you like pleasing me, baby." I groaned, grabbing Rena's hair in my palm. She grasped my legs and squeezed.

"Ugh! Fuck, baby!" I whispered, fell back on the bed, and watched her pop my dick out of her mouth. I wrapped my hand around her neck gently and leaned up to kiss her lips.

"Yes, sir." She kissed down my cheek, across my chest, as she slid down on my dick.

"We have dinner arranged."

"Let's fly back home."

"What about your events lined up?"

I smacked her ass and helped her rock back and forth on my dick.

"Nikki can handle them."

"Are you sure?"

"Positive... Oh God!." Wrapping her wrists behind her back, I pumped faster and faster as I leaned forward. The head of my dick touched her spot. Whenever she squirted, it turned me on even more. I loved to see her face flush in arousal as her eyes dropped low from a high she could only get from me.

"Sante! I love it when you fuck me."

"You handle my dick so well, amore."

She nodded, and I flipped us over with her back on the bed, lifting her legs and keeping them straight in my hands. Her breath hitched, trying to push me back some.

"Never push me away."

"What are you going to do?" she asked, smirking at me.

"This."

I nipped her breast, slid out of her warm pussy, and flipped her to the edge of the bed. Sliding back inside, I thrusted forward as far I could go and stopped.

"Don't stop!" she whined, looking over her shoulder at me.

"Are you going to be a good girl?" I commanded, smacking her ass.

She shook her head up and down, and I kissed up her back to show her how much I missed her.

"All I ever wanted."

"You missed me, Sante."

"Every minute, hour, or day I'm not around you," I confessed, meaning every word. She came again, and I released inside her, slid out, and watched as she fell on the bed, gripping the pillow. I smirked as I walked to the bathroom and picked up a cloth to clean her up.

"To think I hated you before loving you." Rena chortled. I wiped myself and her off and tossed it on the nightstand before crawling in behind her.

Knock! Knock!

"Yeah."

"Dinner is ready, sir," the maid spoke. I blew out a breath and remembered we weren't at my home. Our parents wanted to celebrate the christening of my nephew and have dinner. Rena rubbed a hand over my head, and I kissed the tips of her fingers.

"We'll be down!" I blurted, as I stood, helped Rena out of bed, and went to the bathroom to shower.

"Next time... we send a gift," Rena said, and I chuckled, turning the shower on. Thirty minutes later, we sat around with our family and friends as they talked about her fashion show.

Click! Click!

I stood with my champagne glass, all eyes looking at me. Surprisingly, I wasn't nervous like I thought I would be. In the beginning, I was against marriage and commitment, even though our parents had been married for so many years.

"Savio and McKayla, congrats again for a beautiful

son. I wanted to take this moment to ask Rena Clark if she'll have me as her husband."

Her eyes bucked wide, shocked at my words.

"What did you say?"

"Marry me."

"You want to marry me?"

"Yes, I know it's not the proposal some women get, but I want you forever."

Rena peered around the room at my family, then McKayla. I didn't have time to call her parents to get permission, but we weren't a conventional couple.

"Yes."

I pulled out the ring box from my pocket and helped Rena to stand. My mom and McKayla started to cry.

"Rena, you've been nothing but a challenge since you busted through the doors of Calabresi Inc. I want you to know you'll always have my heart, and I can't wait for you to have my last name."

"I love you so much, Sante." She wiped the tears that pooled in her eyes.

"Me too, baby."

I slid the ring on her finger, rose, and cupped her chin to a kiss on her lips. She stood on her tippy toes and sucked on my tongue.

"Congratulations, Rena and Sante!" McKayla excitedly jumped up from the chair and came around the table to hug us both.

EPILOGUE

SANTE

I glanced at Rena, chuckling at her animated reaction to my nephew throwing up on her shirt as McKayla held him in her hands and cradled his back. At this point in my life, I would be the first to tell my brothers that I would never marry a woman like her. No matter how beautiful, it took more than beauty to capture my heart. Rena challenged me at every moment and fought to be in my life. It was the reason I proposed to her.

"What's up with you and Savio marrying these girls?" Renato grumbled.

I gave his back a squeeze.

"I have no doubt you'll be changing your thoughts of marriage real soon."

He slid his hands in his pockets.

"My life doesn't revolve around love. That's something I'll leave to you two."

Everything my brother had done to keep us safe didn't go unnoticed, and I appreciated the sacrifices as our enforcer that he took. But I wanted him to find someone he could talk his problems out with and fall in love one day to break the hard steel of his heart. Rena being well known for her fashion business set us in a bigger spotlight, but we'd made it work because she wasn't content with only being my wife. Women I'd dated in the past only wanted money and status from me, and I never cared to question because I got what I wanted out of them and moved on to the next warm bed I could find.

"I got the order from Savio we can move forward."

"Be careful."

"If we do this right, we'll be untouchable."

"That's if he doesn't make a mistake."

"What did he tell Rena?"

"She knows enough."

Rena kissed my nephew on the cheek and walked over to us. I wrapped my hand around her waist, whispering in her ear, "You left our bed before I woke up this morning." I bit her ear, smacking her on the ass.

"I'm sorry, I had an early appointment with a client."

"What are you going to do to make it up to me?"

She grinned.

"What would you like for me to do?"

"I see our conversation is finished." Renato waved us off and walked back to the bar with my brother and father. Rena giggled at Renato and buried her head in my chest.

"Renato has that stick up his ass again."

"He's been like that for years."

"I should be happy I got a sensible brother then."

"You should." I smirked, nuzzling my face in her neck.

"McKayla wondered if we could babysit tonight. Savio wants to take her out on a date."

"That's fine, if you're okay with that."

"He can be a little cranky like his uncle, but I wouldn't change that for anything in the world." She pecked my lips.

I lifted her hand with her new engagement ring and kissed the top of her palm. I heard a clear voice and looked over at my mother.

"Rena, I wanted to tell you again... Welcome to the family. We've known you as McKayla's friend, but now as a daughter," Mom announced, holding a glass up in the air to toast.

"Thank you, Mrs. Calabresi. Sante is the best thing to ever happen to me."

"Sante calmed her down a lot. Good job." Renato lifted his shot glass and chugged it down.

"Ignore him," Rena called out, placing her hand on mine. I pecked her cheek, and she grinned.

"I want to make an announcement," Rena remarked.

"Please no more kids," Renato growled, grabbing the bottle of scotch from the bar, and poured in his glass.

"Renato, you could use a good kick in the pants," Rena barked, tossing her hair to the side.

"Renato," I growled, stilling my eyes down at him.

He shrugged and sipped on his scotch, then smirked.

"Sante, you amaze me. I can't wait to share many more years as your wife."

"I feel the same way, baby."

"That's why I want to try for a baby."

"Are you sure?"

"Yes. At first, I was against becoming a mom, but I'm ready."

"You'll be a wonderful mom."

"You'll be an amazing father."

"Here's to our future." She held onto my hand as I leaned down to press my lips to hers as my family clapped their hands.

"Here's to Calabresi's future," she toasted, lifting her arm around my neck.

I HOPE you enjoyed Sante and Rena. Check out the sneak peek of Renato next. Preorder the full novel of **"Renato"** here click the link here. Don't miss the first book in the series **"Savio"** here. https://books2read.com/u/mlEAW7

SNEAK PEEK: RENATO

The night started out as usual, with me finding someone to take care of my needs. The only problem was that I didn't expect any complications or feelings to get involved. As the enforcer of the Calabresi Family, my heart held no love for anyone outside of my parents and brothers. So, tell me why the devil in blue dress that left in the middle of the night reappeared and held a secret I wasn't too sure I could forgive, let alone live with that decision. They say one-night stands aren't for everyone and they may be right, but this second chance brought along something I couldn't keep at bat for long.

RENATO

We'd just finished handling a job, and I needed to let off some steam and decided to hit up the gentleman club that my brother was a part owner of before he got married. I slid through the VIP section and slapped hands with a few of the workers. A few bottle girls smiled at me, but I decided to sit back tonight. Usually, I liked to relieve some stress from a long night with a warm body, but a drink would have to do.

"Boss, did you hear me?" Ian nudged me, passing the bottle of scotch.

"No, what did you say?"

"You want to get some private dancers up here?"

I took the bottle straight to my lips and watched the crowd move in sync to the music from the deejay.

"Not tonight."

"Come on you, always leave a little something."

"Too tired."

"That was a huge score we landed."

Tonight was Ian's chance to handle an enemy of the family who decided to pop up and make some noise. He'd been skimming off the top for a few months and we never caught him after he was told we were looking for him. Tonight, he came back into town.

"Shit!"

I heard him curse.

"What?"

"That dancer over there."

The dark lights covered the left side of the cage she was dancing in. Her breasts were plump, and she had a curvy backside and long legs. I squinted to get a good look because she reminded me of someone.

"Who is that?" I questioned.

"She must be new," Ian suggested. We came here almost weekly if we weren't out working for my family.

She flipped her hair back and wheeled around. I finally saw her face, and my eyes bucked wide in surprise. I jumped up and ran out of the VIP booth and down the steps, pushing through the crowd.

"Boss!" I heard Ian call my name, but he didn't want anything important.

"Argh! Let me go!"

I grabbed the cage door, yanked it open, and pulled her out.

"Shut the fuck up!"

"Help! It's trying to kill me!"

Some of the guards tried to walk up on me, and I pulled my gun out of my side and aimed it at him.

"Follow me and see what happens."

"Help! He's crazy."

"Shut up!"

"Come on, Renato, Do we need to call Savio or Sante?"

For making that statement, I lifted the gun, aimed at his foot, and shot him.

"You're crazy!" she screamed and dropped to the ground. I pulled her to the back exit, shoved her to the wall, and removed my jacket to cover her body. She was only wearing panties and tassels on her breasts.

"Please let me go," she pleaded.

"Where's my money?"

"Renato, I'll get it for you."

"I want it now."

"I can get it out of the bank tomorrow."

I pressed the gun to the side of her head.

"Either you give it to me right now, or I will kill you."

"Please, no! I... I... get your money. Just don't hurt me."

"Tell me why I should spare you?"

"Because I...!

Pop! Pop!

UPCOMING RELEASES: 2022/2023

Sante

Renato

Elio Jr.

Vincenzo

ABOUT THE AUTHOR

L.K. Ryan is an author of Romantic Suspense, Dark Romance, and Contemporary Novels. Join my newsletter and sign up for the latest news and updates on my books and releases:

CALABRESI MAFIA SERIES

Savio: Book 1

https://books2read.com/u/mlEAW7

Sante: Book 2

https://books2read.com/u/mdd1oW

Renato: Book 3

Elio : Book 4

Vincenzo: Book 5

Thank you so much for reading. If you enjoyed the crazy ride and decide to leave a review, we'd appreciate the support.

Acknowledgments

Readers that keep me motivated and show love for my crazy characters and want more.

www.ingramcontent.com/pod-product-compliance
Lightning Source LLC
Chambersburg PA
CBHW011159190726
48286CB00009B/2842